GOOD SON, BAD SON

Seth Grainger hoped that his sons, Scott and Leo, would inherit the ranch he dedicated his life to, making it one of the biggest in Wyoming. But when Scott becomes the prime suspect in a murder, is Leo really being the good son when he sets out in search of his brother? Trouble looms for the Grainger family: Seth struggles to keep his family together, but faces the prospect of a double tragedy and a dilemma of unimaginable consequences.

BILL WILLIAMS

GOOD SON, BAD SON

Complete and Unabridged

LINFORD
Leicester

First published in Great Britain in 2011 by
Robert Hale Limited
London

First Linford Edition
published 2012
by arrangement with
Robert Hale Limited
London

British Library CIP Data

Williams, Bill, *1940 –*
    Good son, bad son. - -
    (Linford western library)
    1. Ranchers- -Fiction. 2. Fathers and sons
    - -Fiction. 3. Brothers- -Fiction. 4. Western
    stories. 5. Large type books.
    I. Title II. Series
    823.9'2–dc23

    ISBN 978–1–4448–1097–4

Published by
F. A. Thorpe (Publishing)
Anstey, Leicestershire

Set by Words & Graphics Ltd.
Anstey, Leicestershire
Printed and bound in Great Britain by
T. J. International Ltd., Padstow, Cornwall

This book is printed on acid-free paper

1

He had made up his mind that he would head home tomorrow unless his luck changed. Now he had an uneasy feeling as he pulled his mount up beside the faded sign that read BRUNSWICK TOWN and, in smaller letters, Harlan Bryce Brunswick 1801–1852 RIP. It was the large notice pinned to the sign that attracted his attention; it read:

KEEP YOUR GUN IN ITS
HOLSTER
by order of
Marshal Ed Stockman.

He had been told that this town was full of trouble and it seemed the sort of place that would attract his brother and the kind of men he would mix with. He urged the sorrel forward, but kept it at walking pace as he entered Main Street.

The dusty street was wider and longer than in most towns, and the buildings he was passing were mostly of the solid brick construction common in the big cities. The Marlborough Hotel was impressive, standing on its own and looking too grand for ordinary folks to be able to afford to stay in. A smartly dressed doorman was brushing the fine white horse that was hitched to the highly polished carriage with the hotel name on the side in gold-coloured fancy lettering. As he rode further into town many of the timber buildings were showing signs of neglect and reminded him of those he'd seen in a shanty town. Passing the boarded-up Gilhooley's and then the Mavericks' saloon made him wonder whether the town had hit hard times, or might there be an active temperance movement operating here? He was relieved when he saw that Minty's saloon was open and the two cowboys who had just staggered out were propping each other up as they headed towards the diner across the street.

He was close to the saloon when he spotted two men sitting on a bench. One of them nudged the other before nodding in his direction. The man might as well have said, 'That's him' or 'We're in luck', such was his body language. They were an unsavoury pair, unshaven, probably unwashed and downright mean-looking.

He dismounted near the hitch rail. His feet had barely touched the dusty ground when a voice came from nowhere 'We'll mind that fine horse for a dollar, mister.'

Grainger whirled around and saw the two boys who had started coming down the steps of the saloon. The older one was about fifteen, stocky and black-haired and he had a cheeky grin. Grainger figured he was the one who had spoken. The other boy was likely three or four years younger, fair-haired, slightly built and looked shy as he lowered his eyelids.

Leo Grainger was twenty-three years

old, slim built, fair-haired and his thin features were mostly set in a serious expression. He couldn't help thinking that the two boys were not unlike what he and his elder brother, Scott, must have looked like ten years ago.

'I think my horse will be just fine, boys, but thanks for offering,' he replied, his face showing his amusement. The cheeky one shook his head as much to say, 'big mistake', and looked in the direction of the two mean-looking characters whose eyes were fixed on Grainger's horse.

'I guess this is your first time in our little ol' town, mister, and you mustn't have heard about the horse-thievin' that goes on here. I noticed that fine animal of yours hasn't been branded and it could attract the attention of some like those two.'

The boy had nodded in the direction of the two men who were now having a conversation. Grainger looked across the street at the marshal's office. He'd planned to call in there later and also make a call at Jerome's undertaker's, which was next door, just like he'd done at every other town to which he'd paid a visit, to see whether his brother might be in the cells, or the cemetery.

The cheeky one saw him looking across the street and told him that the marshal was out of town. Then he added, 'The deputy marshal will have gone fishing, or he'll be hiding in the back office. Either way the door will be locked, because he's a chicken-livered coward. A dollar doesn't seem much to make sure your horse is there when you want to ride out of here. Anyway, we'll be getting along because we've got chores to do because if we don't earn some money then our three little sisters won't be eating much tonight.'

Grainger didn't believe a word of the sob story, but he just didn't trust the two men nearby who were probably the boy's older brothers, so he called them back after they had started to walk away. He reached into his waistcoat pocket and handed the quiet one a dollar.

'You've just made a wise investment, mister. Now you can enjoy your beer without any worries,' said the cheeky boy. He turned to the quiet lad and asked, 'Isn't that right, brother?'

The quiet one didn't reply and Grainger made his way up the saloon steps wondering whether his horse would still be there when he came out.

Before he'd left his home a month earlier to search for his brother, Scott, he had never even been in a saloon. Now he had lost count of those he'd entered, hoping to find someone who could help him. He brushed his clothes, using his hand and Stetson to flick away the dust, and was about to push open the swing doors when he read the sign offering a free sample of whiskey with the first beer. Any thoughts that trade must be poor were soon gone when he entered the crowded bar. At least he didn't get 'the stranger in town look' that he'd experienced most times. The room was thick with smoke and stank of stale puke that would have masked the cheap perfume that the saloon girl who winked at him was wearing. His thoughts were suddenly of Emma and what lay ahead for him. Dear sweet Emma, who didn't deserve all those lies they told about her and her menfolk. Perhaps some women were just jealous of her beauty.

He made his way to the space at the bar that had just been vacated by a cowboy who looked as though he had drunk too much and who hurried towards the door to save the embarrassment of puking on the bar room floor. Grainger didn't need to turn around to know that the cowboy hadn't made it outside.

'What'll it be, stranger?' asked the curly-haired barman, who was cleaning a glass. He hadn't bothered to remove the large cigar from his mouth while he spoke.

'Just a beer,' Grainger replied. He wasn't much of a drinker, having seen what trouble it had got his elder brother into.

'I'm afraid the free whiskey offer ended ten minutes ago. Sorry,' apologized the barman with a shrug of his shoulders.

'The whiskey's like water and the beer's like piss,' one of the cowboys advised, belched and then swayed before he reached out and grabbed the bar for support.

The barman exchanged some banter with the drunk when he replied, 'You never could take your booze, Murdoch, and now you even get pissed on water.'

Grainger smiled, but didn't bother to tell the barman that he never touched whiskey.

He still didn't feel at ease in a saloon and he was uncomfortable as he waited for the beer and surveyed faces within his view, hoping that his brother might be here. Some men looked away while others held his gaze and their expressions didn't show any signs that strangers were welcome. The group sitting at the nearest table looked a motley bunch and the big feller with unruly hair and a bushy beard spat on the bar room floor. Grainger suspected that it was meant to send a signal to him. The hostile action had him thinking that perhaps he would drink up and leave, but he had ridden a long way to get here. He decided to take a risk and enquire about his brother, but he would bide his time. He sipped his beer and kept looking towards his reflection in the mirror behind the bar, careful to avoid any further eye-contact that might trigger some hostility. When the friendly barman asked him if he was just passing through he pulled out the crinkled Wanted poster and asked in almost a whisper if he had ever seen the man. Grainger could vouch for the likeness that had been captured in the sketch on the poster.

'You'll have to speak up, buddy. I can't hear you above the noise that rowdy bunch are making,' advised the barman as he nodded towards one of the tables. Grainger repeated his question in only a slightly louder voice, but it had coincided with a lull in the noise close by. The barman looked worried, then leaned forward and lowered his voice as he started to offer Grainger some advice, but he was only part-way through giving it when Grainger felt a heavy nudge in his side.

'Bounty hunters ain't welcome in this town, stranger,' the man growled, causing his spittle to land on Grainger's face. He could smell the whiskey from the man's hot breath. It was the bearded man who had spat in his direction earlier.

'Don't go causing trouble, Jacko. This feller is only passing through and maybe that wanted man deserves to be caught. He might be a woman-molester or even a killer.' The barman hadn't noticed that the man named in the poster was wanted for a killing, but he hoped that his attempt to pacify the town's chief troublemaker might just work. Jacko had been the cause of more blood being spilled on the saloon floor than any other man in town.

'This man's my brother,' Grainger explained, sensing that serious trouble might be coming his way.

'What sort of man would hunt down his own brother for a measly reward? I just don't like you, mister. I thought you had a sly look as soon as I set eyes on you.'

Grainger glanced towards the table and saw the other members of the group stand up and they presented him with their meanest looks. If they intended to frighten him then they had succeeded.

'I can see me being here upsets you, mister, but my brother is innocent. I am trying to find him so I can tell him that our pa is dying and wants to see him. I'll just finish my drink and leave.'

'That's a very touching story, asshole, but I am betting it's a load of bullshit. If you're planning on leaving then why don't we just help you on your way?' Jacko sneered.

'All right, I'm going,' Grainger quickly replied as he stuffed the Wanted poster inside his shirt, sensing that there was no way this man could be reasoned with. He pushed his unfinished beer away and turned to leave, but Jacko had signalled to his two buddies, who had now moved closer to him. Grainger put his hands in front of him in a submissive stance and repeated again that he was leaving, but it didn't stop Jacko from splitting Grainger's cheek wide open with a vicious head-butt. He stumbled and would have fallen to the floor, but was helped on his way when one of the men who had picked up Grainger's glass from the bar smashed it in to Grainger's right eye. Some of onlookers winced and instinctively backed away. One young cowboy who had never seen a brawl before started retching and puked down the front of his new silk shirt that he'd worn to impress the saloon girls. Led by Jacko the three men took turns in delivering a boot in to the semi-conscious Grainger's body and face and the sickening thuds echoed around the otherwise silent saloon. A few men walked away in disgust, but no one was prepared to intervene.

It was only the sound of the shotgun being cocked that made the men stop and turn to face the barman, to discover that the weapon he was holding was pointing at them.

'That's enough, Jacko. Just back away before you kill that feller. You all leave now, or I'll send someone to fetch Marshal Stockman and I'll hold you here until he arrives.'

Jacko delivered a final boot into Grainger's bloodied face before he took heed of the barman's warning and indicated to the others to stop. The warning had come too late to save the sight in Grainger's eye caused more by Jacko's spur than the damage caused by the broken beerglass. The watery mush that had once been an eye was spread in streaks down his cheek, but some strands still connected through the gaping hole.

'Jesus Christ,' the barman shouted

out, jumping over the bar as the saloon door closed behind the last of Jacko's thugs. He pulled off his barman's apron and tried to stem the flow of blood before ordering some of the onlookers to help carry Grainger over to Doc Sweeney's surgery.

2

Duke Bradley had only been drowsing when Grainger was carried into Doc Sweeney's surgery. His own body ached and his broken nose was throbbing from the beating he had received from a couple of the 'heavies' in the saloon after he slapped one of the girls because she had complained about him being smelly. Bradley winced when he saw the bloody face of the new arrival and again when the man's shirt had been ripped off by the doc.

'Is he dead, Doc?' Bradley enquired, but turned his gaze from the man. Bradley was squeamish when it came to the sight of blood, even though he had spilled that of others more than most men had.

'No, he'll live, but he'll have trouble attracting a woman,' replied the doc. The doc knew that his patient wasn't hearing about how his future prospects with women wouldn't be good and the comment was made in sympathy and was not a cruel jibe. The man's face had suffered hideous injuries, but the doc had seen even worse ones during the war. As always, he hoped that he would have the guiding hand of the man whose identity he had taken.

Samuel Corps had been orphaned as a young boy and became a drifter until he enlisted for the Confederates in the middle part of the Civil War. He was badly wounded during a battle near Sonning Fields and was unable to rejoin his unit, so he stayed and assisted the doctor who had attended to his wounds. The doctor was General Surgeon Roland Sweeney and they became good friends. During the time he worked alongside the surgeon he learned so much that towards the end he was encouraged to act as a doctor. Roland Sweeney came from a wealthy family and he promised Samuel Corps that he would help him become a qualified doctor. Then tragedy struck. Roland Sweeney had been preparing to amputate a soldier's gangrenous leg when the demented soldier grabbed a gun from the nearby table and shot him at point blank range. Sweeney died in Samuel Corps's arms. His dying words had been, 'You can be me, Samuel.' Samuel Corps didn't know what his friend had meant, but it gave him the idea of adopting the surgeon's identity after the war. He even displayed the certificates on the wall that were among the surgeon's personal belongings. Roland Sweeney's family were in Ireland and he had few friends, so Corps was confident that if he moved far enough away from Cedar Valley where Roland Sweeney had lived before the war he would never be found out. He hadn't taken the surgeon's identity for financial gain, but because he had reasoned that his patients would have more confidence in him if they believed he was a fully qualified doctor with grand framed certificates on his surgery wall to prove it.

Doc Sweeney's impostor was forty-two years old. His small ginger moustache was tinged with grey and his chubby face was almost the colour of a ripened red apple, due to the effects of liquid comfort. The doc's liking for hard whiskey had started when a young girl in his care had died from an infection after he'd treated her for injuries following a fall from her first pony. The girl's death was not his fault, but he had carried the burden ever since. His trips to the saloon and the hoards of whiskey he held for medicinal purposes had helped him. Surprisingly the drink had seemed to give him a steadying hand when he was attending to bad injuries, or at least it had in the beginning. Now his hands had developed a permanent tremor, although his patients were often unconscious, too traumatized or drunk to notice.

The doc was pleased when Grainger started to come round before he had started the serious work of patching up his face. He reached for the small mug that he'd filled with laudanum earlier, lifted Grainger's head off the pillow, and offered the mug to his lips.

'Come on, young feller. You need to try and get some of this down you, because I'm afraid that what I need to do is going to be really painful even when I've finished.' He wasn't sure whether Grainger understood what he'd told him, but he sipped and then gulped the liquid through his swollen lips and muttered something, but it was too garbled to understand. The doc soaked part of the large pad he was holding with chloroform. Although he was wearing a surgical mask he always instinctively held his breath, lifted his head high and turned it away whenever he was administering chloroform. He held the pad against Grainger's face long enough for it to have worked, then put the pad on one side, ready to soak some more and use again if Grainger indicated he was conscious enough to be feeling the pain. The doc carefully removed the soft materials he'd placed on the open wounds to stem the flow of blood and cleaned around the lacerations with a solution that was made up by mixing red-oak bark with water to act as disinfectant and assist the healing process. The laudanum would help when Grainger came out of his unconscious state. The doc was almost ready to start his work.

Doc Sweeney had worked alongside some doctors in the war who didn't believe in any form of anaesthetic because they held the view that the patient needed what they called the 'shock element' to aid their recovery. Grainger would have reason to be thankful that Doc Sweeney's mentor had never believed in the 'shock element' theory.

The doc had taken the precaution of giving Bradley a whiff of chloroform because he didn't want his patient's constant jabbering to disturb his concentration. He took a large gulp of whiskey, gave a deep sigh, then he gently removed the jelly-like substance that had once been

Grainger's right eye and placed it in a small dish. He covered the hole with a pad, then reached for one of the threaded needles, ready to begin stitching together the various open wounds, starting with the right ear which was hanging like a flap. As the needle entered the reddened skin, Grainger pulled his head to one side and cried out with pain, causing the doc to stop and give his patient another sniff of the chloroform-impregnated pad and then help himself to a gulp of whiskey. The doc had taken the added precaution of tying Grainger's body to the bed with strips of cloth, so that when he resumed the stitching Grainger remained mostly still and the painful cries were more subdued.

★ ★ ★

The doc was drained after his prolonged concentration when he decided that he'd helped the poor man to the best of his ability and inspected his finished work. He had gained some experience in the war, but he was not the most skilful when it came to knitting together pieces of torn flesh. In recent months he had suffered pains and stiffness in his hands, a condition he had seen in some of his older patients. He knew that the scars would be more unsightly than they might have been, but he had done all he could and now it was up to nature. It was the mental anguish that would cause this young man grief and even misery. An unsightly scar could give a cowboy a hardened look that made men wary of him because they believed it must be the result of a brawl. Grainger's injuries would likely only cause him to be pitied and more likely mocked. It was a sad fact of human nature that some people tried to make up for what they believed were their own inadequacies by picking on others.

Duke Bradley came out of his chloroform-induced state and felt the throbbing pain. He gently rubbed the bridge of his nose, but pulled his hand away when he felt the squashy feel and clicking sound of pieces of bone. He should have paid the measly five dollars even though the painted whore hadn't given him any satisfaction and she'd been mouthy when she mentioned him being smelly. He'd been told that most women found a man's body sweat attractive and manly, not realizing that it was his breath, which smelled like he had the remains of dead maggots lodged in between his few remaining teeth, that she'd mostly complained, about.

Bradley had been wondering what he was going to do. The arrival of the badly beaten stranger had given him an idea. He would be praying that the feller didn't die, because they might be able to help each other.

★　★　★

When Grainger woke his head was pounding as he ran a tongue over his dried lips. He could smell the remains of the strong whiskey that the doc had forced him to drink when he was semi-conscious and it took him a while to recall what had happened. At first he could remember riding into town and that was all, but slowly the full horror of his beating returned. He struggled to open his eyelids and when he did he couldn't see anything on his right-hand side. He passed his fingers across the right side of his face and cried out when he discovered the hole where his eye used to be. He slowly used his fingers to explore the rest of his badly swollen face, but stopped when he touched the broken cheekbone, which made him cry out again. He had noted his missing teeth and a nose that was no longer straight but bent to one side.

He turned his head towards the direction of the sound of snoring and saw the thin face of a man who had his mouth open. They had one thing in common and that was a broken nose. Grainger was about to turn away, having noticed that the foul smell coming from the man was stronger than the whiskey, when the man opened his eyes and sat up. 'Jesus,' he shouted out, 'your face it's . . . ' Bradley paused, unable to find the right words. But it wasn't because he wanted to spare Grainger's feelings, so he continued, 'Did you fall in front of the stagecoach or was it a train?' and didn't bother to hide his amusement at his own remarks.

Grainger told him through badly swollen lips that he had taken a beating, but the man who introduced himself as Duke Bradley already knew that from what the doc had told him. Grainger found Bradley's continuous talking, accompanied by regular sniffs, annoying and he just wanted to try and sleep again because then perhaps the pain would go away. He was relieved when Doc Sweeney came in and enquired how he was feeling, but before he could answer Bradley started talking again, this time to the doc.

'Hey, Doc, are all those certificates on the wall there your . . . what do they call them . . . qualifications?' The doc was preoccupied with examining Grainger's swollen face and there was a delay before he replied, 'They're my medical certificates that prove I'm a qualified medical man and entitled to call myself a doctor.'

The doc didn't show any discomfort when he lied about the certificates and he proceeded carefully to peel back the dressing on Grainger's cheek. Then he turned to the large shelf behind him and took a small bottle from it.

'Hey, Doc, are you sure you ain't a witchdoctor? I was having a bit of a nose around this morning when I got up to use the piss-pot. I was reading the labels on some of those bottles. Why have you got that stack of leaves, bits of bark and strange-looking plants in those boxes over there?'

'I'm afraid I am just an ordinary doctor, but I served in the sad war that was fought between our brave country-men from both sides. There was a severe shortage of medicines and drugs so we had to produce substitutes using those materials that nature provided. Some of them are better that what the drug makers produce and they are much cheaper.'

'But you ain't no ordinary doc if you make your own medicine with those plants and herbs,' Bradley said, trying to flatter the doc, hoping he might remember the compliment when he came to settling his bill. He also had another question to ask.

'My pecker felt as though it was on fire last night after you put that potion on it. What did you say that thing I have is called? I mean the fancy name, not pox.'

The doc gave a wry smile and told Bradley the disease was syphilis. He had noticed that when Bradley was brought in with his nose injury he kept scratching around his manhood. The doc didn't tell him that he had treated it with just a mild disinfectant that he had made up from some of the items in the basket and that it wasn't going to help him very much.

'It will get better, won't it, Doc?' Bradley asked, showing more concern for what he thought was a simple itch than his broken nose. The doc lied when he told him it would, but warned him once again not to go with any saloon girls until it had completely healed. He didn't have the heart to tell him that his condition was too far gone to be cured and that he would probably go blind and perhaps mad before he died, long before his time.

'Well, I hope it's gone when I leave here, because you've just made me feel horny mentioning saloon girls.' Bradley laughed, then had yet another question to ask. 'Doc, I guess you having all those qualifications means you're going to be charging me and this dude more for fixing us up?'

The doc smiled and told Bradley that he only charged his patients what they could afford. He knew that his two current patients could pay him in cash, unlike the last one who had given him a saddle. The man had been beaten up because he had been caught cheating in a card-game after he had gambled and lost his horse. The saddle was stored in the back room of the surgery along with a vast assortment of guns, buckles, Stetsons, watches and all manner of things that cowboys had given in payment for their treatment in lieu of dollars they didn't have. One cowboy had offered the doc his wife for a month and he'd been serious.

The doc had been making one of his special concoctions in a small mug while he was talking to Bradley. Now he helped Grainger to sit up and offered the mug to his lips.

'This will help dull your pain. It also contains some nutrients, but you might feel like some solid food later.'

Grainger whispered his thanks to the doc. Within a few minutes of the doc leaving he had drifted off to sleep, while Bradley was still cursing whoever the saloon girl was who had left him with the pox. Grainger didn't hear him say that he had no intention of leaving the saloon girls alone just because he had a little itch and a painful pecker.

3

Leo Grainger didn't like Duke Bradley, but before Bradley had left Doc Sweeney's surgery he'd told him that he knew where his brother was and he would take him there. Bradley had seen the bloodstained Wanted poster displaying an artist's impression of his brother's face and his name when the doc had put it on one side after he'd stripped away Grainger's shirt to attend to his injuries. The mere mention of his brother reminded Grainger that if it wasn't for him he wouldn't have been here. He hadn't been surprised to learn that his brother had joined up with what he would discover later was a notorious gang. The gang had killed thirteen men, mostly stagecoach drivers and bank tellers.

The most daring raid had been when they burst into the Dillon saloon in

Crombie Falls and took all the money from the gambling tables, made the customers empty their pockets and hand over any gold rings or watches they had. While the posse was out pursuing them they had sneaked back into the town and robbed the secure building where gold was bought. They had shot a man between the eyes as soon as he had opened the safe. The gold had been moved on the previous day and the safe had only contained a tiny nugget that wouldn't have paid for more than a few slugs of whiskey. It was not worth the loss of an innocent man's life. Bradley had said that he needed Grainger's help with something first, then he would take him to his brother.

★　★　★

Grainger had mixed feelings when Bradley turned up at the surgery just as he was preparing to leave. It had been three days since Bradley had left and Grainger had done a lot of thinking.

31

'You still don't look too good, mister, but perhaps a good helping of grub over at the Fat Cow's diner is what you need. Isn't that right, Doc?'

Doc Sweeney was thinking that it would take more than food to solve Grainger's problems. He had been disappointed that a simple test had revealed that what was left of Grainger's badly misshapen ear wouldn't be of any use to him because he couldn't hear anything through it.

'Just make sure you keep those wounds clean and nature will take care of the rest. Fresh air and sunshine can help the body heal better than most medicines. Best to wait a few days before you start wearing the eye patch I gave you.'

The doc had tried his best to be positive and didn't mind lying if it helped the poor wretch.

Before the two men left, the doc invited Grainger to come back and see him before he moved on so that he could give him a final check over. He'd given Grainger back the small wallet that he'd retrieved from inside his shirt when he was brought to the surgery. He only charged him a modest sum, just to cover the cost of the medicine, materials and the whiskey the doc had consumed during his treatment of Grainger.

Once the two men were outside the surgery, Grainger shielded his remaining eye from the bright sunlight and asked Bradley where they were heading.

'We'll be staying at an old cabin just outside of town until we do our little bit of business. I asked the deputy what happened to your horse and he knew nothing about it, said it must have been stolen. I hope it wasn't anything special, but don't worry, we'll get you a horse tomorrow. Mine is tied up by the cabin, so we'll mosey on down there now, then we can discuss my little plan.'

Grainger had some vague memories of talking to some boys about his horse, then he remembered paying them to look after it. He figured they must have taken his money and his horse.

Bradley hadn't lied about it being

just a short walk to their temporary home; it was situated amongst three others and close to the cemetery. Grainger's first thought was that he hoped it wasn't going to rain because the cabin's roof contained a few large-sized holes. The inside was no better. The blankets on the double sized bed looked grey and soiled with spots of blood. He grimaced when he spotted several bugs jumping, perhaps in anticipation of some fresh flesh to bite. He shook his head to rid the thought he'd just had of the bugs feeding off his leaking wounds.

Bradley had made some coffee on the fire that had been about to go out before he'd met up with Grainger. He picked up a dirty metal mug and threw the contents that had been left in it on to the floor and then filled it with lukewarm coffee. Grainger shook his head when he offered him the mug, so he took a gulp of it himself and then began explaining his plan.

Grainger had been musing over what Bradley might have in mind, but he wasn't prepared for what had just been proposed. When Bradley asked him what he thought, he replied without hesitation, 'You can count me out.'

'Well, that surprises me, mister, but perhaps you don't want to see that brother so badly after all and you got your face all messed up for nothing.'

'I won't stand much chance of finding him if I end up in a cell,' Grainger snapped back with a show of irritation as well as disappointment.

'Forget it then, because maybe you are too chicken-livered for the job. I guess you wouldn't fancy coming up against that feller Jacko again who made a mess of your ugly mug.'

Grainger's wounds seemed to hurt even more just at the mention of the man, and he asked Bradley where Jacko came into it.

'Jacko is employed by the bank as a private security man because the bank has had more than its share of robberies. Doc Sweeney told me that the bank hasn't been robbed for over six months and it was probably because word had got out that Jacko was employed there. Jacko has killed four men in his so-called line of duty, but two of them were innocent. Jacko is a trigger-happy son of a bitch.'

Grainger was confused as he tried to decide what to do. Much as he hated the man who had changed his life, that wasn't the main reason he was thinking of changing his mind.

'I might be interested, but I need to know how you know where my brother is. And I need to know that there won't be any killing. I'm not going to hang from a rope if things go wrong.'

'Your brother is holed up with the Mackenzie gang in a hideaway not too far from here. Mackenzie sent me to check out the bank, but I figure with your help I can do the job and then head back and give Mackenzie and the boys a big surprise when they see the loot. There's a lot of money spent in this town, mostly from the cattle boys stopping off here when their herds are driven across the Galton Plains.'

'OK, maybe when I've rested up here for a week I'd be prepared to think about it,' said Grainger, but he was in for another surprise.

'We need to do the job tomorrow and no later, because Mackenzie will think something has gone wrong. He'll move on and I'll have trouble catching up with him and you'll never find your brother. So, I need an answer from you now. If it's a no then I'm out of this dump of town. I'll tell your brother that you were looking for him.'

'I'll do it,' replied Grainger after he'd weighed up Bradley's long-winded explanation. He added, 'But I won't kill anyone if it goes wrong, not even that feller Jacko, tempting though it might be.'

'You aren't a lot like your brother, mister, but I guess he wouldn't let Jacko do what he did to you. I saw him beat the hell out of two fellers off a cattle drive who tried to muscle in on a saloon girl he fancied. He sure has a temper.

The two men were out cold on the saloon floor and he pulled out his pistol. We all thought he was going to finish them off proper, but he seemed to change his mind.'

'How did he get involved with your gang?'

Bradley sniggered, showing his set of tobacco-stained and chipped teeth before he replied.

'It isn't my gang and I don't think Mackenzie would be too pleased to hear you say that. Mackenzie and Grainger are pretty close even though Grainger is new to the gang. He hasn't been with us on a robbery yet and this was going to be his first. I'm not even sure how they met up, but my buddy reckons that Grainger was in a bar when a brawl broke out and he sided with Mackenzie. I guess they're two of a kind, being evil bastards who would kill their own grandma for money.' Bradley sniggered again when he added, 'But you probably know that already, or maybe she's still alive.'

4

Grainger hadn't slept much as he'd tried to get comfortable on the hard floor, not wishing to share a bed with Bradley and the bugs.

Bradley had left just after dark and gone to the saloon. It was daylight when he tried to creep in to the cabin. His efforts were wasted when he knocked over a chair and didn't bother to lower his voice when he let forth a barrage of foul language as he rubbed his painful shin. When he saw that Grainger was sprawled on the floor he gave him a muttered apology for not coming back last night with some food like he'd promised. He blamed his absence on Lucy, the saloon girl who had the biggest titties he'd ever seen.

'She was a bit special and I swear she would have done it for nothing the way she was sighing and groaning even when I'd hardly started. They would have heard her groaning in the bar below if it hadn't been for the piano player making his own racket.'

Grainger didn't want to hear the details of Bradley's night with the girl, but he got the full account right up to the moment that Bradley had left the girl on the bed begging him to come back tonight. Grainger remembered seeing a saloon girl shortly before he was set on by Jacko who would have fitted Bradley's description, except she was old enough to be Bradley's ma and Bradley must have been at least thirty-five years old. Bradley eventually stopped talking about other women whom he had pleasured, and sniggered when he said that there must be lots of little Bradleys up and down Elmore County.

'If it wasn't for my liking of women I could still be living back in Buffalo Plains where I was born and raised. I put little Jenny Crook in the family way and her pa came looking for me.

Started insisting on wedding bells and all that shit. I would have sent him packing, but Jenny's got seven brothers and a couple are as mean as they come, so I told old Magnus Crook that I wanted to marry his sweet daughter and I left the next day. I ain't been back since and I never will; but I sure miss the place and my kinfolk. I've got a couple of cousins that must have blossomed into real beauties by now.'

Bradley stopped yapping and placed a small bag that he'd brought with him on the table. He took out some biscuits and a small loaf of bread which he handed to Grainger, then he pulled out a fancy watch from his shirt pocket. He'd stolen the watch from a man who had been sleeping on a bench on the sidewalk when he'd first arrived in town. When he'd finally worked out what time it was he had some instructions for Grainger.

'The bank will be open in just over an hour, so best get some grub in your belly and we'll saddle up, make our way into town and leave the horses in the gap between the bank and the general store. I brought you a horse back from town last night and hid it out back. It's buckskin and a bit on the skinny side, but it'll do.'

Bradley paused while he yawned and Grainger asked him why he hadn't called in the cabin last night and told him about the horse.

'I guessed you'd be asleep so I headed back to the saloon. It probably belonged to one of the bunch from the cattle drive who were in the saloon, but I heard them say they were moving on at sunup, so they'll be gone by now. There shouldn't be too many people about, but try and not be seen because they aren't going to forget a face like yours. Don't worry; I managed to get us a large neckerchief each to cover our faces when we hit the bank.'

The cruel comment had been delivered with his usual smirk, and Grainger was reminded of the grotesque face that he'd seen in the cracked mirror he'd

42

found in a cupboard last night. His hopes that Bradley would stay quiet while he ate his food soon disappeared.

'I forgot to mention that your old buddy, Jacko, was dishing out another beating last night. The kid was only about eighteen, maybe less. It was probably his first time in a saloon. Jacko had this girl sitting on his knee. They call her Mimi and she's supposed to be French, but if she's French then I'm a Chinaman. She's a real tease and knows how to get a man's attention. She was all over Jacko, rubbing herself against him and stroking him. I had a good view and it made me horny and I would think just about everyone else who was watching. She caught my eye and winked and gave me a look that said, 'Would you like some'. The young kid was real close to her and Jacko and he was ogling her. I bet his mouth was dry and he was feeling funny like you do as a kid. Jacko saw him having a good look and pushed Mimi to one side and started roughing up the kid. Made a real mess of his face, but nothing as bad as yours, although he lost a few teeth and his nose looked all over to one side.'

Grainger was reliving his own beating as he listened and was glad when Bradley finished the tale by saying that the girl told Jacko that she liked him being jealous. She'd led Jacko upstairs while a couple of men had helped the kid to his feet and then to Doc Sweeney's surgery.

When Grainger mentioned that he had something to do before the robbery, Bradley wasn't too pleased and growled at him when he told him what it was.

'I wouldn't bother buying the old doc any whiskey. Some say that he distils his own out at an old property near the Conway River.'

The doc wasn't one of Bradley's favourite people after what he'd done in the saloon last night and spoilt the plans he had for a saloon girl. Bradley had told Grainger a pack of lies about bedding Lucy. He had been making arrangements with her when the doc had beckoned him over and told him that if he tried to take any of the girls upstairs then he would tell Linda, who was in charge of them, about his disease. So Bradley spent the night drinking and scowling and his mood wasn't helped when he'd watched Mimi doing her teasing when she was rubbing her body against Jacko before they went upstairs.

Grainger insisted on buying doc the whiskey and rode the buckskin on the short distance in to town. The street was deserted and no one else was in the general store when he bought the two bottles of what the storekeeper had told him was the doc's favourite. The doc's surgery was in semidarkness when he crept in and he was disappointed to find the doc sound asleep, so he just placed them by his side. The young feller lying on the bed looked at Grainger and pulled the sheet over his face in a cowering manner, but not before Grainger had seen the effects of Jacko's latest act of brutality.

Bradley was sprawled out on the bed when Grainger returned to the old cabin, but he got off the bed, yawned and started scratching. This time it was his chest and not his usual place of discomfort.

'Damned bed bugs,' he growled as he continued scratching, then he addressed Grainger.

'I thought you might have done a runner, but maybe you've got more guts than I thought.' Bradley looked at his stolen watch and announced that it was time to go. He suggested that Grainger ride on ahead and he would follow behind. They would meet up in the side alley that separated the bank from the general store.

While Grainger waited for Bradley to appear he was having serious doubts about going through with his part in the robbery because he just didn't trust Bradley. He had just tightened his grip on the reins and was preparing to spur his stolen horse forward when Bradley appeared. Sensing Grainger's uncertainty he delivered a warning.

'Don't think of backing out, mister, because you know too much and I'd be obliged to make sure you never talked, if you know what I mean.' Bradley tapped his pistol, to make it clear that Grainger was either in or he was dead.

'I told you I'm in,' Grainger snapped back, hiding his nervousness with a flash of aggression.

Bradley had promised Grainger a modest cut of the robbery money and suggested it might come in handy to buy the services of a saloon girl whose eyes weren't too good. Grainger was getting tired of Bradley's constant reminders about his face, but figured that it was Bradley's way of compensating for his own ugliness, which was an act of nature and not brutality.

'Right, let's cover our faces,' Bradley ordered. He pulled his blue-and-white neckerchief from inside his waistcoat and tied it to his face.

Grainger had cut two holes in his neckerchief, He struggled to adjust it, but eventually he managed it. He dismounted from his horse and tethered it alongside Bradley's dark-brown mare, using the same wooden support.

The Brunswick bank had been started by Archibald Dwyer and his brother Sidney, who was the businessman of the partnership. They had been born into a banking family in Drover City and started their working lives as tellers at the biggest branch of the Union State Bank. Sidney had seen the business opportunities when Brunswick was an expanding town whose economy had been fuelled by wealthy ranchers, buffalo-hunting, and gold-prospecting in the tributaries that ran down from the mountains and flowed into the Melrose River. Archibald had been reluctant to form a partnership with his brother, but had been swayed by the family doctor's advice that his wife Alice, who suffered from breathing difficulties, might benefit from the clean air out West. The partnership had prospered until Sidney suffered a fatal heart attack nearly five years ago. Since then some of the bigger ranch owners had moved their accounts to a big bank in the next town. Archibald was content to operate on a smaller scale and spend more time with his ailing wife.

Jacko was leaning against the wall just beside the door inside the bank, thumbing through the pages of the newspaper even though he couldn't read. He'd been drinking heavily with his buddies last night and Mimi had given him a parting present before he had rolled out of her bed a little over an hour ago. He planned to get himself some breakfast later and a pot of coffee to help liven himself up. He hadn't even bothered to look up when the door had first opened. When he saw the two men with their faces covered he was too slow to react and reach for his weapon before Bradley poked his own Colt 45 in to Jacko's flabby belly.

'You'll be sorry,' Jacko snarled in a

lame threat. His fists were clenched and he was embarrassed for being caught on the hop by two dudes whom he was certain he could take on with one hand behind his back.

'Don't even think about blinking, or I'll put a bullet in that ugly mug of yours,' Bradley snarled. He moved his face to within an inch of Jacko's while holding his pistol barrel close to Jacko's cheek. Bradley laughed as he added, 'By the way, you forgot to wash your whore's lipstick off your face.' Jacko instinctively wiped his hand across his face to remove the legacy of Angie, the saloon girl who always applied more make-up than the other girls. Angie was no spring chicken and the heavy make-up helped hide the ravages of time. Mimi had suggested that they invite Angie to join them after they had finished their first bout of love making because she wanted to watch Jacko and Angie performing. He hadn't been keen, but Mimi had convinced him that he wouldn't regret it and he hadn't.

'I said, don't move,' Bradley snapped and positioned the end of his pistol close to Jacko's right eye. Bradley yanked Jacko's pistol from its holster, then ordered Jacko to sit on the floor. Jacko glowered at him as he sat down and muttered something between clenched teeth when Bradley told him to put his hands on his head.

'Just don't try anything, fat boy, and we'll soon be on our way.' Bradley laughed and added, 'I was going to call you big man, but one of the saloon girls was telling me that you ain't so big where it matters. I guess nature can be real cruel.'

Jacko's face reddened. The veins stood out on his neck and he was on the verge of lashing out at Bradley, but thought better of it, conscious that the other robber was also pointing his pistol at him.

Bradley stepped away from Jacko and told Grainger to keep him covered. Then he turned his attention to the bank manager. 'Now you, mister, need to start filling up a sack with as much money as you can because if it's not enough then you won't be seeing your little wife ever again. Now get those fingers moving and bag all the money you've got.'

Archibald Dwyer was a small man, but his frame seemed to shrink even further as he fumbled to obey the order. His eyes couldn't hide the fear he felt as he looked at the barrel of the pistol that was pointing at him. The man who had just threatened Jacko sounded evil and it was likely that his threats were real and not bluff or made just to frighten. He had heard tales of robberies, but in all his years in banking he had never witnessed one, even though they had happened at his own bank when he had been away. He wondered if the robbers had kidnapped his dear wife, Alice, whose life had just been threatened. Despite his sorry predicament his thoughts turned to the hardworking folks whose money had been entrusted with the bank. There would be no compensation for them and the loss would likely ruin some. Joe Lacey had recently deposited the money he was saving towards some new farming equipment that he needed if he was to survive another growing season. Bob Holder had called in just yesterday with the proceeds of his trip to the cattle market and the money was to go towards his daughter Rosemarie's wedding. Archibald blinked to clear his tearfilled eyes, then he thought about the pistol that was kept under the counter. He'd never fired it before, but he wondered if he could live with himself if he didn't try and do something. Then his thoughts turned again to Alice, who depended so much on him. He pulled back the hand that had been slowly edging towards the hidden weapon, knowing that he wouldn't get the pistol into a firing position before he turned Alice into a widow. He hoped that he wouldn't have to convince himself later that he hadn't been a coward.

Archibald managed at last to fill the bag that was now bulging with a quantity of dollar bills that exceeded Bradley's expectation and prompted him to say, 'You're a sensible man, mister banker.' Then he turned to Grainger and said, 'Let's go.'

Jacko had been studying the robber who hadn't spoken. When he noticed the specks of dried blood on his waistcoat he made a stupid mistake and blurted out: 'You're the bounty hunter. I know you.'

Grainger glared down at the man who had changed his life for ever. He was about to speak when he was deafened by the sound of Bradley's gun, which had delivered two shots at Jacko, splattering parts of his face and brain on the wall behind where he had been sitting.

Bradley turned towards Dwyer, 'Sorry, mister, but big-mouth there just cost you your life.' Bradley used his pistol to gesture towards Jacko's body which had fallen back against the wall. What was left of his face was on full display.

'Please don't. I've done what you

asked and I won't tell the marshal anything,' Dwyer begged and then repeated, 'Please don't.' As the tears rolled down his cheeks he made one final plea, which was a simple, 'Please, my wife is sick and she needs me.'

Bradley studied Dwyer, sighed and said, 'All right, because you have co-operated, little man, I'm going to let you off, even if it means that folks will think I'm really a bit of a softie.'

Bradley headed for the door as Dwyer was thanking him for his mercy, but when Bradley swung around he saw the relief on the little man's face turn to horror just before he fired one shot into his face and another into his body as he fell back.

Grainger recovered from his state of shock and glowered at the merciless killer beside him.

'You had no need to kill that poor man,' he roared at Bradley, who just smiled at him. Then he pushed Grainger towards the door and out on to the sidewalk.

Grainger was still thinking of the scene inside the bank and was fumbling with the reins of his horse when Bradley, already mounted, heeled his mount into action. Bradley's horse was into a full gallop down the dusty main street before Grainger started to give chase. He saw the owner of the general store come out of his store, then hastily retreat back inside; otherwise there had been no reaction to the shooting. But when he glanced back he saw someone running across the street from the marshal's office. It was the deputy and he was about to discover the carnage in the small bank, the inside of which was now splattered with blood.

Grainger wasn't able to catch up with Bradley. By the time they had ridden a few miles out of town he was beginning to think that he had been tricked, until he saw that Bradley had pulled up his mount and was waiting for him. Grainger was nervous and he wondered if he was about to become the third victim at the hands of a man whom he'd watched kill two men in cold blood. He pulled on the reins and eased his horse into a slow trot as he approached the smiling Bradley, who had just taken a whiskey bottle from his lips. Grainger lowered his hand towards his pistol handle, hoping that the gesture wouldn't be seen by Bradley. His thoughts drifted to his pa's advice to him and his brother when they growing up, which had been to get in first. Pa's philosophy was that the element of surprise could compensate for lack of skill with fists or a pistol. His brother had found that both had come naturally to him, but Grainger had always been slow and clumsy.

'You did all right, mister, for a first-timer. I might suggest that Mackenzie lets you join the gang. You could team up with your brother.' Bradley took another swig from the whiskey bottle and for a moment Grainger thought this might be his best chance, but perhaps Bradley really did know where his brother was. Grainger felt reassured by Bradley's praise, but he was soon to realize it wasn't sincere when Bradley roared with laughter, making it clear that he was mocking Grainger.

'You could scare the bank tellers and stagecoach drivers with that face of yours. You might even be able to stop a train with it.'

He didn't bother to reply to the insult or when Bradley suggested that he should be grateful to him for killing Jacko.

'I lied when I said the camp was close by. It's a good hard ride from here, but just in case a posse comes after us it's best if you ride on a bit while I leave the trail here. I'll wait for you while you double back and meet up with me. It might just confuse them if they think we have split up if they look at the horse tracks.'

Grainger followed Bradley's instructions and rode off but when he'd travelled far enough he turned to look and was surprised to see Bradley beckoning to him, because he expected Bradley to have ridden off. He was in for another surprise when he rejoined Bradley who drew his pistol from its holster and ordered him to ride in front. Bradley looked deadly serious when he said that MacKenzie would kill him if he thought he had brought a bounty hunter into his camp.

5

Grainger's stolen buckskin seemed to have got its second wind as it galloped ahead of Bradley, but both horses were breathing heavily when Bradley ordered him to slow down. The sky had turned dark with heavy rain-clouds that seemed to have appeared from nowhere. They were riding at a gentle trot when they approached a large wooded area and Bradley shouted out that they were getting close. Grainger glanced over his shoulder and was greeted by the smirking face of his tormentor, who waved his pistol threateningly.

'This is just a precaution, because I've been thinking that you don't look much like the man you claim is your brother. I don't really believe that bullshit about you wanting to find him to tell him that your pa is dying either.'

Grainger didn't bother to reply to

what was a statement of fact. Scott favoured his pa's looks and Leo had always felt weedy next to his brother, even though he was no midget. Grainger's hair was fair, just like his late ma's, while Scott had the thick, curly hair of his pa and grandpa, whom he remembered seeing laid out in his coffin when he was a small boy.

He felt nervous and the tension rose in him when Bradley ordered him to turn his horse towards a small clearing and said that they were almost there. The rain had come with a vengeance and although it had eased, it was still dripping from their Stetsons. Grainger had heard Bradley curse his horse as it had slipped in the muddy trail and threatened to unseat him while he was trying to light a damp cheroot.

'You'll soon be reunited with your brother, unless you're up to no good, mister. If you are, then the man you claim is your brother will make sure that you wish you had never been born, and you won't need to worry about looking like a freak.'

Grainger realized that he had made a big mistake agreeing to enlist the help of Bradley. He had ended up in big trouble because two men were dead and he had been part of it. He turned nervously when he heard some movement in the bushes, but Bradley told him to relax because it was Mackenzie's men looking out for unwanted visitors to their camp.

Bradley was feeling pleased that they were about to enter the camp, anticipating the surprise that Mackenzie and the gang members were about to get when he told them he'd already done the robbery. They could head straight for Hyatt Falls and all have the night in bed with a saloon girl instead of spending another one sleeping on hard ground and only have memories of their last woman.

'It's me, Bradley, and I've got a visitor,' Bradley called out. He slid from his saddle and gestured with a wave of his pistol for Grainger to do likewise.

'Lead your horse through that gap in the trees and remember I'll be right behind you.'

Bradley led his own horse while keeping his pistol pointing at Grainger's back as they entered the camp. Two men were sat by a fire that was spluttering from the light rainfall. A partly skinned carcass of a medium-sized animal lay near by attracting the attention of a swarm of flies that buzzed around it. One man, who would have dwarfed Jacko, stood up and began hurling abuse at Bradley. Grainger figured the man must be Mackenzie, who had been sitting next to his brother.

Mackenzie made a threatening move towards Bradley and raised an arm to strike him, but pulled back when the bag of stolen money appeared at his feet. He still gave Bradley a string of abuse and threats before he stared at Grainger.

'Who's this freak and why are you pointing a gun at him?'

'It's a long story, Mack, but perhaps our buddy Grainger can tell us,' Bradley said, accompanying his reply with his usual snigger. He holstered his pistol and then reached for the coffee pot that was brewing on the fire, which was now just glowing embers, the flames having been extinguished by the rain.

Scott Grainger looked up, his face showing a puzzled expression as he pointed at Leo and said, 'Huh! What's he got to do with me?'

Leo was surprised and confused by his brother's remark before he announced, 'Scott, it's me, Leo. I've come looking for you because Pa is dying and he wants to see you. He wants to make his peace with you.' Leo had sounded desperate as Mackenzie's scowl had intensified.

'What's your game, mister?' Scott asked angrily. Then continued with another question. 'Is this some sort of a joke, because I don't have a brother and never have. My pa was killed in a shoot-out in some place I can't remember when I was thirteen years old.' Scott shook his head. Then he asked, while looking directly at his brother, 'What happened to your face, mister?'

Bradley seemed bemused by the exchange, but replied for Leo with his own explanation.

'He was asking about you in the saloon in Brunswick and when he pulled out your Wanted poster, he got more than he'd bargained for. You didn't tell us that you were wanted for a killing, Grainger.'

'There are lots of things you don't know about me, Bradley, and you're not likely to seeing as how you are a blabbermouth,' Scott Grainger replied while looking Bradley in the eye.

Bradley was too thick-skinned to be affected by the comments. He continued telling what happened.

'Anyway, some of the locals heard him enquiring about you and figured he was a bounty hunter. A feller by the name of Jacko did most of the damage. I sort of took pity on him and offered to bring him here if he helped with the robbery. I figured I was doing you a favour, Grainger, and I thought I was doing him a favour when I shot Jacko during the robbery. I thought it best to get rid of the little banker feller as well. He got on my nerves squealing about his little wife.'

'So, you dumb-ass, you brought us a bounty hunter and you killed two men,' Mackenzie growled. 'I ought to — ' Mackenzie's threat was interrupted by a voice that boomed out from the bushes and brought shocked expressions to the faces of all those gathered by the fire.

'This is the federal marshal and we have you surrounded. Throw your weapons down and place your hands above your heads and we'll let you live.'

Mackenzie glowered at Bradley, figuring that the marshal and his men had followed them into the camp. He whipped out his pistol from its holster and fired in the direction of the caller, preferring to die from a bullet rather than dangle from the hangman's rope.

He'd watched too many men turn blue and choke to death while a gathering of ghouls looked on with morbid curiosity. He'd even known men who would ride over a hundred miles just to see someone swinging from a rope.

Bradley was the first to fall to the ground when a bullet hit him in the throat. His blood sizzled as it sprayed on to the fire. One of the posse had saved Mackenzie a job, because the gurgling sound from the gaping wound had stopped and Bradley was dead. The firing was rapid and not very accurate, as the posse were effectively firing blind as they hid behind the trees. The next bullet to find a target thudded into the upper part of Leo Grainger's chest. He pitched forward on to the lifeless body of Bradley. His brother showed no emotion.

'Let's get out of here,' shouted Mackenzie. He raced towards the nearer of the two horses that had been led in by Bradley and Leo Grainger. He was already settled in the saddle when

Scott Grainger placed his foot in the stirrup that dangled from the buckskin. The shots continued to rain down on the camp and another one hit the groaning Leo Grainger in the leg. None reached Mackenzie and Grainger, who got clear of the camp and were soon galloping away, relieved to see that the posse hadn't covered that side of the camp.

Federal Marshal Jimbo Jenkins had waited a few minutes after the return fire had stopped, then he ordered his men to follow him into the camp.

'Shit,' roared the marshal when he saw just Bradley and Grainger lying on the ground covered in blood and realized that Mackenzie and one of his gang had escaped on the horses belonging to the two men who had been shot up.

'Damn, shit,' he roared again. The posse had left their horses away from the clearing and crept up on foot in case their animals snorted or neighed, giving them away as they approached

68

the gang's camp.

'Make sure those two are dead,' Marshal Jenkins ordered his chief deputy. A few seconds later he was answered with a nod of the head. They'd also shot dead the two lookouts when they tried to make a run for it, so Jenkins ordered his men to go and retrieve some spades off their horses and dig some graves in the softest spot they could find.

'We could carry the bodies into Brunswick when we take Dooley in to have his wound attended to and return that money to the bank,' said the marshal, pointing to the large white bag with *Brunswick Bank* written on it.

'The gang's horses must be tethered close by and we could use them to carry the bodies back to town, but I don't fancy doing all the paperwork or making the local undertaker any richer than he is. Two graves will do and don't bother burying them too deep. It will be hard shit if some scavenger digs them up.'

Dooley had received a bullet in the shoulder and was feeling sorry for himself. He wished the marshal had just left the dead men to the vultures so he could get to see a doc sooner.

6

Scott Grainger and Mackenzie had pulled up beside a small lake, figuring that they had put enough distance between them and the posse if the marshal had decided to come after them. They had no way of knowing whether they had inflicted any casualties amongst the posse when they returned their fire. Grainger hadn't slept much, but it had nothing to do with seeing his brother clutching his chest near the bullet wound that was spurting blood though his fingers. The disfigured face had managed to show a look of hatred that he'd never seen before. The brothers had never been close and Grainger didn't really know why, except maybe it was because of Leo's odd jealousy and the fact that he'd always been a loner. Scott Grainger had done things he regretted; now his brother was probably dead and he needed to do some serious thinking.

It had been a mistake to join Mackenzie's gang, but he had just got drawn into it. He needed to see his pa, and then there was Emma. He'd had his share of saloon girls and some had been special, like Annabelle back in his hometown of Bordon Valley, but Emma was different. He knew that Emma had feelings for him and perhaps she might even have been drawn to him because of his wild streak. He had known women who were attracted to bad and even evil men. Some would harbour a killer if they were besotted enough!

By the time Mackenzie had stopped snoring and grunting in his sleep, Grainger had lit a small fire and brewed some coffee from the supplies he had found in the saddlebag attached to the buckskin.

Mackenzie rose from his makeshift bed of a blanket covering some soft leaves and began badmouthing Bradley again for bringing the posse to the camp.

'The dumb-ass had his suspicions

about that freak, so I don't know why he fell for that bullshit that you were his brother, but at least he got what he deserved because him and Bradley ended up dead.'

Mackenzie sipped on his coffee before he placed the mug near the fire and lit up a small cheroot that he pulled out of his top pocket. He took a heavy drag on it, coughed, spat on the fire, then said that they would have to decide where they should move on to.

'It's a pity we couldn't have grabbed the money from the bank robbery that Bradley had brought back,' said Grainger, thinking that a share of the money would come in handy for what he had plans for.

'Yeah, I was thinking that,' Mackenzie agreed. 'I think we'll probably head for Hyatt Falls. It's about a day's ride from here and the last time I was there they didn't have a marshal. Do you know it?'

'Never been that far east, but I've heard of the place. The thing is, Mack,

I've been doing some serious thinking about some personal business I need to take care of back in Bordon Valley.'

'Is that where you're from?' Mackenzie asked. 'You never did say.'

Grainger nodded and hoped that Mackenzie wouldn't press him too hard on his reasons for going back, but it wasn't to be.

'What can be so darn important that you'd pass up the chance to see some action in Hyatt Falls? I've got a bit of money left over from the last job I did, so we can have us some fun.'

'There's a woman back there who I just can't get out of my head. I have to see her again and try persuading her to come away with me.'

'I didn't have you down for a sucker, Grainger. There are plenty of women in Hyatt Falls. But if you're determined to go to Bordon Valley then I'm coming with you. We can think about doing a job there. I take it they have a bank in the town?'

'Not a very big one,' Grainger replied

and hid his disappointment that he wasn't going to get rid of Mackenzie as easily as he'd hoped.

'We're not greedy.' Mackenzie laughed, then scowled when he asked if they had a lawman.

'Charlie Stephens was the marshal when I left. He's a bit long in the tooth, but he can handle himself and he's probably still got a couple of young deputies.'

'It doesn't sound like it's anything we can't handle. So let's get moving just in case that federal marshal is still on our tail, and let's hope we can pick up some grub along the way.'

Grainger could only hope that Mackenzie would change his mind and forget about going to Bordon Valley. Otherwise he might have to think of a way of getting rid of him.

7

Deputy Marshal Cas Fogle was sitting in Marshal Stockman's seat when the imposing figure of Federal Marshal Jimbo Jenkins appeared in front of the desk and asked where the marshal was and whether there was a doctor in town.

The deputy was flustered as he explained that the marshal was away and that Doc Sweeney had a surgery further down on the other side of Main Street, but added that he was probably in the saloon.

'I've got a wounded deputy outside so you and one of my men take him to the surgery. You can go and drag the doc out of the saloon if he isn't where he should be. I expect he's sniffing around the saloon girls if it's the same horny feller who I saw the last time I was in this sinful place.'

Fogle hurried around to the front of the desk, eager to follow his orders, but before he opened the door the marshal had some more instructions for him.

'Make sure you hurry back here, Deputy, and lock up the prisoner I've brought in for you. He's one of the two villains who robbed your bank. He'll be wanting the doc as well, but it's probably a waste of time. He's already had a practice run in a grave and would have been buried alive if he hadn't started groaning when he was being buried. He was lying on top of his buddy because my dumb-ass deputy said that he was dead, but he was coughing up soil and puking by the time we dragged him out.'

★　★　★

Doc Sweeney sighed when he saw the pale face of the man he never expected to see again. He wasn't happy attending to a patient in the cells which still had the smell of urinals, but the deputy said that it was for the prisoner's own good because feelings were running high after the two deaths in the bank robbery.

Doc Sweeney ripped open the shirt and saw the old bloody dressings he'd applied a few days ago. Carefully he examined the new bullet wound before cutting away the leg of the pants to reveal the second wound and saw that the bullet had shattered part of the shinbone.

'You may not believe this, feller, but you are darn lucky because neither of those bullets is lodged near anything vital. I'll dig them out in no time at all. It looks like you must have banged your head when you fell and that would account for you being out cold and the lawmen thinking you were dead. From what they told me you were covered in soil when you first groaned and you had one heck of an escape. You're going to feel sore later, but I'll be giving you a big swig of whiskey to help ease the pain. I guess you're familiar with the procedure by now. By the way, thank ye kindly for leaving those bottles of whiskey for me. The young feller who was in my surgery described who it was who left them.'

Grainger had thought his mind was playing tricks on him when he'd remembered being pulled out of a hole and then looked down and seen Bradley's dead eyes staring up at him. Now he was thinking he was dreaming as he heard bits of the doc's familiar voice.

Doc Sweeney delved into his large black-leather medical bag and took out various bottles and jars containing laudanum, chloroform, home-made anti-septics and finally a large bottle of whiskey. He placed the needles that were already threaded with fine silk strands close at hand, ready for him to stitch the torn flesh together. He always prepared the needles in advance when his shaking hands were not too bad. It wouldn't have done the patient's confidence much good to see him struggling to thread the needle, even though he had no problem seeing the narrow slit in the needle.

The deputy who had been enlisted to hold the lamp spent most of the time with his head turned away or his eyes closed as the doc went about his business of digging out the two bullets and then doing his stitching. Grainger started to react to the pain of the needle into his flesh towards the end and the doc applied the chloroform-soaked pad against his face and then took his customary healthy swig from the whiskey bottle before he completed the job.

The doc gathered his instruments and various bottles and jars and placed them back in his case while he was instructing the deputy to make sure that Grainger was given plenty of water. The doc also suggested that the deputy should think about giving the cell a good clean after he had mopped up Grainger's blood that was splattered around the cell floor.

★   ★   ★

Leo Grainger felt a throbbing pain in the back of his head as he tried to shake the fuzziness from his brain. He remembered hearing Doc Sweeney's voice and when he opened his remaining eye he expected to see the familiar sight of the doc's surgery, but he didn't. He eased himself up and felt pain from the fresh wounds in his chest and leg and found himself staring at the bars of his cramped cell. His head began to clear and he remembered hearing a man talking to the deputy. The man must have been the federal marshal and he'd told the deputy to tell Marshal Stockman that he owed him a favour for bringing in one of the bank robbers and burying the other. Grainger let out a groan when he realized that his worst fears had come true and he was going to hang.

The deputy, who had checked on him throughout the day and brought him food, told him that Marshal Stockman would be back in the morning. He didn't seem interested in

Grainger's pleas that he hadn't been the one who had shot the two men in the bank and warned Grainger that there could be trouble when word got out who he was and explained why. Archibald Dwyer had been a popular man, but there wouldn't be too many tears shed for Jacko who had even been feared by members of his little gang, but they could still cause trouble if they got fired up with whiskey. Grainger had instinctively touched his swollen face at the mere mention of Jacko and the other men who had been responsible for his beating. He wasn't reassured when he was told that the office would be locked, but not manned overnight, nor did he like being told to make sure that he peed in the pot and not on the floor.

★ ★ ★

By the time sun-up came he had hardly slept as he had listened to the noises outside, not knowing whether they were cowboys in high spirits, just letting off steam, or troublemakers who would soon be breaking into his cell. He had tried to take the doc's advice not to move unless necessary, but he had been restless and the chest wound hurt like hell.

When Deputy Fogle arrived with his modest breakfast of beans and bread, Grainger had no stomach for food, but the hot coffee was welcome and it helped remove the dryness from his mouth. The deputy had handed him a shirt and pants that the doc had brought over last night on his way to the saloon; he hadn't mentioned that they had belonged to a man whom the doc couldn't save. Grainger protested his innocence once more, but the deputy just shrugged his shoulders when he asked him what was going to happen to him.

'The federal marshal said that you confessed to holding up the bank and he seemed to think that you'd hang for that because two men died, but I guess

Marshal Stockman will know what the procedure is. There hasn't been a hanging in the town since I arrived here just over a year ago, but we do have a courthouse. I'm not sure where they'll hang you, though.'

8

Marshal Ed Stockman had listened carefully while his deputy briefed him on the robbery and the arrest by the federal marshal and felt a mixture of sadness and anger when the deputy had finished telling him.

Ed Stockman was sixty years old and stood an impressive six foot two inches. His nose was broad and been broken four times; the eyes were weary and yet probing, and his thick mop of greying hair was almost shoulder length.

Marshal Stockman had been a preacher before he became a lawman. The loss of his first wife, Mary, and three young daughters to the fever had been too much a test of his faith. He'd turned to drink and brawling before the previous marshal had told him to stop wallowing in self-pity. That had been twenty years ago and now he had a new wife and his life was good.

'It's a real shame about old Archibald Dwyer,' the marshal said with a sigh and then continued:

'Folks say that bankers are cold and calculating, but he always showed sympathy and understanding when it came to farmers who were in trouble and needed more time to repay a loan. I'll pay Alice a visit later and see if she needs any help with arranging the funeral, but I expect Fergus Jerome has already been and done that. Fergus and Archibald were like chalk and cheese because old Fergus sees every burial as a business opportunity, no matter how sad the circumstances. I had to send him packing a few months ago when he came calling and asked my Bridget if she had thought about what sort of coffin she would like me to be buried in when the time came.'

'For what it's worth, Marshal, the doc said this feller Grainger didn't strike him as the sort to get involved in a robbery. It seems that he was just looking for his brother and that's how he ended up being nearly beaten to death by Jacko and his buddies. I ain't ever seen anything like the mess his face is in.'

'I'd better have a talk with him later,' replied the marshal.

'Oh, I nearly forgot to mention that the federal marshal said that when they were watching the Mackenzie gang's hideaway that feller was led in at gunpoint, so it didn't seem that he was a member of the gang.'

* * *

Grainger turned his head away from Marshal Stockman after he'd gingerly stood up from the cramped bed, when the marshal had arrived at his cell and beckoned to him. The pants supplied by the doc were three inches too short and only added to the pathetic figure he presented, but at least the chest wound had stopped throbbing.

'I'm Marshal Stockman and I want

you to tell me exactly why you came to my town, robbed a bank, and why you ended up in the camp of the notorious Mackenzie gang. If you start bullshitting then I'll leave. I'll be sending a wire to Judge Oakley in Kelso City later today so that we can get your trial arranged, and you'll need to have an attorney.'

Grainger repeated himself a number of times as he explained things to the marshal about how he got involved in the bank robbery. When he'd finished the marshal gave him a long, sceptical look. He couldn't help but pity Grainger for what he'd been left with after his beating and being buried alive, but there was still a possibility that he was either a killer or a very, very good liar.

'I'm finding it hard to believe that you would risk a hanging just to find this brother of yours, who is a nogood. When the jury sees your face they aren't going to believe that you weren't the one who fired into the face of Jacko, so it won't matter none if you didn't kill poor old Archibald.'

'But I've never killed anyone and I don't think I could,' Grainger pleaded. 'I told Bradley I wanted no part in any killing and he promised me that there wouldn't be any. I swear to God, Marshal, it happened just like I said.'

'So tell me again: why you are looking for this brother of yours who is a wanted killer?'

'My pa is dying. He might already be dead because I've been searching for my brother for a month. This was going to be the last town I would try and find him and then I was going home to look after Pa.' Grainger felt his face as he said, 'With respect, Marshal, I am sorry I ever set foot in your town and that's the truth as well.'

'Some men would disown a son who had killed another human being,' the marshal commented as he recalled the various killers he had come into contact with and the reaction of their families. Some were ashamed and it had ruined their lives, but others would never turn their back on kinfolk no matter what they had done.

'I think Pa blames himself for the way that my brother turned out. He passed off my brother's wild behaviour as just being high-spirited, but my brother is evil. I know things about him that Pa doesn't, but I didn't want to destroy a dying man's image of his son.'

Stockman held eye contact with Grainger, trying to decide what sort of man this wretched-looking individual really was. Eventually he concluded that he agreed with Doc Sweeney's opinion. Grainger wasn't a bank robber; more likely a decent human being who had been in the wrong place at the wrong time. Grainger would end up losing his life just because he tried to carry out his father's dying wish. That wasn't justice in Stockman's book.

* * *

Marshal Ed Stockman pushed away his plate which still contained most of his dinner. The gesture brought a troubled look to the face of his wife, Bridget.

'Is it my cooking, or is something bothering you, because it's the first time you've not left a clean plate in all the time I've been cooking for you,' Bridget said jokingly to mask her concern.

Stockman gave his wife a weak smile and apologized. 'Sorry, honey. You must make the best meat pie in the whole of Wyoming and just about anywhere else. It's that feller we have locked up for the bank robbery. I have a feeling that he's been one unlucky man and got caught up in something that wasn't of his making.'

'Is the poor man's face as bad as folks have been saying?' Bridget asked, her homely, smooth-skinned face showing her sympathy.

'It couldn't be much worse. I've seen some horrible injuries from bar room brawls, but nothing close to being as bad. It's not just his injuries, but he just seems a broken man. I've told the deputies to make sure that they don't leave him with anything he might use to end his own life, but you could hardly blame him if he did.'

Bridget sometimes wondered whether her husband was just too caring to be a marshal. Yes, he was as tough as they come, but he had a sensitive side that he kept hidden and he worried about people in a way that others wouldn't. She would be glad when he retired, but until he did she would support him. She suggested that perhaps he might feel like finishing his dinner later and reminded him that there would be his favourite apple pie and custard to follow.

'I won't let it go to waste, honey, and I'll feel more like eating when I get back from the office.'

'Your deputy won't take kindly to you checking up on him when it's your night off. Why don't you stay and have a few glasses of that whiskey you were given by the mayor?'

The marshal was already on his feet and heading towards his gunbelt hanging by the door. He told his wife that he wouldn't be gone long, then he could relax and have the whiskey after his meal.

Bridget kissed him on the cheek and shook her head as she watched him leave. She did worry about him and the dangers he put himself in, but she knew that he loved the work even though he wasn't always appreciated by some folks who took him for granted. She wished that his deputies were a bit older and more experienced so that they could share the load.

'Have you changed your mind?' Bridget asked when her husband reappeared.

'No, honey, I forgot something. I won't be gone long.'

Bridget's face looked troubled again when she saw him leaving with the item he'd forgotten. It was his trusty double-barrelled shotgun that he'd nicknamed Daisy, but he didn't know why and it prompted his wife to say with a forced smile, 'So you're taking your other woman for a walk.' Stockman smiled back and stepped outside.

Stockman nodded to his neighbour, Joel Benson, the town's blacksmith. The big man was taking in the cool night air as he leaned on the white wooden gate in front of his house, puffing on his clay pipe.

Joel took the pipe from his mouth just long enough to say, 'Evenin', Marshal.' Joel was a man of few words, his favourites being 'yup' and 'nope'.

Stockman lived far enough from the centre of Main Street not to be disturbed by the noise that was always likely in a town like Brunswick, but as he reached the first of the stores he heard the sound of voices in the distance. That wasn't unusual at this time of night. There were always some rowdy cowboys who took in more liquor than they could handle, but they rarely caused any serious trouble. Most of the brawling was usually over a saloon girl and as to who would be the first to go upstairs with the most attractive one, or at least what they thought was attractive through whiskey-clouded eyes. Many would see the girl in the cold light of day and feel embarrassed that they had fought over her and ended up spending a night in a cell.

Stockman was musing over Grainger as he walked and thinking what the man's future might be if he was to avoid a hanging, including his prospects for marrying. He had always found it strange how men and women were attracted to certain types when choosing a partner. Many men would prefer to sleep with a saloon girl rather than a churchgoing girl whom they would like to marry. In the same way some women were always attracted to bad men and often regarded law-abiding and good men as boring. Human nature was a strange thing in Stockman's experience. Maybe even Grainger could find some happiness.

Stockman forgot his creaky knees and ran when he saw the door of his office wide open and a body lying on the sidewalk outside.

'Damn, damn,' he roared out, blaming himself for not realizing that something would happen. He mounted the steps to the sidewalk, knelt down beside the unconscious Deputy Fogle and lifted his head off the floor. There was a gash on the side of the deputy's face and a trail of fresh blood trickling down his cheek. Stockman was relieved when the deputy started groaning and, although groggy, he told the marshal what had happened.

Stockman dragged the deputy and propped him against the front wall of his office, satisfied that he wasn't badly hurt, then he picked up the shotgun he had leaned against the wall. He crossed the street to the general store hoping that he wouldn't be seen, then hurried along the sidewalk towards Minty's saloon. His prisoner, Leo Grainger, was standing on a cart that had been positioned near the entrance to the saloon and there was a noose tied around his neck. One of the late Jacko's buddies, Mikey Devlin, was trying to loop the other end of the rope through a wooden support that held up a large wooden sign bearing the saloon's name in large blue letters. Mort Hitchen was seated on the cart, ready to lash the whip that would have the horses pull the cart away and leave Grainger hanging below the sign as the life was choked out of him. Urged on by Jacko's best buddy, Earl Dobie, the mob began chanting, 'Jacko, Jacko.'

Leo Grainger was barely conscious but still able to realize the full horror that was in store for him. He'd been dragged from his cell, had his hands bound, his shirt ripped from his body, and been pulled along the street by two ropes that had been tied to the saddles of two horses whose riders were full of whiskey and eager for revenge. Some of Grainger's old wounds on his face and the one on his chest had opened up. His body was a criss-cross of red streaks where the skin had been ripped off and his pants were bloodied in places where they had been torn by loose stones mixed in with the sand of Main Street.

Stockman hadn't been seen by the mob until he appeared in front of the saloon. He drew his pistol and fired into Mikey Devlin's hand, causing the man to drop the rope and squeal like a pig. The bullet had passed through his hand and his blood trickled down the inside of his sleeve as he held his arm up, too afraid to look and see whether he had lost any fingers. Stockman holstered his pistol and levelled his shotgun at the mob, who had been shocked into silence.

'I'll shoot anyone who makes a move for a weapon and that's a promise,' Stockman growled while training the gun directly at Earl Dobie.

'We were going to save the town the expense of a trial and a hanging, Marshal,' Dobie roared back at the marshal, then he added, 'Why don't you go home and pretend you didn't see anything?'

'Now you listen up good, Earl. You move this rabble out of here now and I might just forget about locking you up for assaulting my deputy.'

Dobie hesitated for a moment, not wishing to lose face in front of the men to whom he had promised a hanging, but he knew that the marshal wasn't one for making idle threats. His hand hovered above his pistol, but bravery wasn't his strong point and he wasn't about to risk the marshal shooting him at point-blank range. He'd wanted to do the right thing by Jacko, but he wasn't about to die for him.

'We'll be going, Marshal, but if the jury don't find that no-good bounty hunter guilty,' Dobie nodded towards Grainger who looked as though he was about to collapse, then continued with his threat, 'we'll finish what we started here before you interfered.'

Dobie turned and made his way up the steps to the saloon. The rest followed except Mikey Devlin, whose face was still twisted in agony as he scurried away to Doc Sweeney's surgery with blood dripping from his hand. The mob had kept a wide berth of the marshal, who'd adjusted his rifle to keep Dobie covered as they filed into the saloon.

Deputy Fogle had been covering the marshal from across the street, having shaken off the effects of the blow to his head. Now he came over with his pistol still at the ready. The marshal enquired if he was all right, then they lowered Grainger down from the cart and stood at either side of him while they helped him across the street to the cells.

* * *

Grainger cowered in the corner when he heard the door to the area where the cells were open. He feared that he was going to be dragged out again, but Doc Sweeney had called to attend to his latest injuries.

'You haven't been blessed with much luck, stranger. I would seriously think about changing your guardian angel.' Doc Sweeney's attempt at a little humour was lost on Grainger.

The doc bathed his wounds with a cloth dipped in one of his specially prepared solutions and the cell soon smelt like a hospital. Each dab of the cloth made Grainger grimace in pain and when his broken cheekbone was gently touched he cried out in agony.

By the time the doc left Grainger was thinking that perhaps it would have better if the mob had finished the job they started.

9

Stanmore Poulson briefed his assistant once more as he stood on the platform of the Ewshot Junction railroad station. He was determined to make sure that his wife Elizabeth and daughters Clare and Isobel were escorted to their seats on the train to Drover City. The Poulson family had been visiting Elizabeth Poulson's sister and her husband had taken the opportunity to attend to some railroad business. He would have already left on the train to Morgan County to attend an important business meeting by the time the train that would take his family in the opposite direction to Drover City had arrived.

Poulson had no real interest in the railroad other than as a business venture and had invested heavily in the Mid-West Rail Company. He had recently been appointed its president.

He was one of a number of men who became known as robber barons: men who were utterly ruthless in business, prepared to bend the laws and in some cases break them if it meant earning a profit. The robber barons had their critics, but some would say that without their vision and risk-taking the West would not have been opened up and thrived the way it had. In their own way they contributed as much as the brave pioneers who toiled in the fields, on the ranges, working in harsh and dangerous places and none more than the men who laid the many miles of rail track. It was to be a proud day when the first Transcontinental Railroad, originally known as the Pacific Railroad, was established. The linking of the rail networks was marked during a special ceremony in Utah on 10 May, 1869 with the driving of a golden spike into the track. It would bring about a great influx and movement of people and result in dramatic and lasting benefits to the economy of the great American West.

Some of Poulson's board members were enthusiasts and passionate, but although he lacked their passion his vanity allowed him to show his pride when the board had voted to name the newly constructed bridge that crossed a narrow section of the Crookham River after him. He reminded his wife to make certain that his daughters were awake when their train approached the Poulson Bridge. Sometimes he wished he had a son to carry on the name, but he loved his daughters very much and hoped that one day they would marry into a good and rich American family.

George Coplan, the stationmaster at Ewshot Junction, had been nervously hovering in the background when the Poulson family were saying their good-byes. Coplan had been dreading today ever since he'd received the details of Poulson's trip and had spent a restless night wondering whether Stanmore Poulson was as bad as the reputation he had for giving rail workers a hard time with his unreasonable demands.

Coplan was a small man standing at five foot seven inches, clean shaven, with narrow features and eyes that might have suggested that his family had some Chinese connection had it not been for his fair skin and hair. As always his uniform was immaculate and a new army recruit at the Mallory Military Academy would have been proud of his highly polished boots. Poulson had been civil enough when he introduced himself, but his snooty wife had given Coplan a look that suggested that he had stood in some horse manure. Her two daughters had giggled at the mention of his name and had continued to find him a source of fun. He'd decided that it was probably on account of his cap, which had been provided by the company and was intended for someone with a much larger head than his.

Coplan heaved a sigh of relief when he saw Stanmore Poulson's train pull out of the station. The rest of the Poulson family would be going to the finest hotel in town before returning to the station to board their train to Drover City, due to arrive in just over two hours' time. He had just witnessed the last time the Poulson family would ever be seen together.

10

Thomas Larkin had worked for the Mid-West Rail Company ever since it had opened four years ago and had welcomed the change from riding shotgun on the various stagecoach routes. It had seemed a so much safer job in the beginning. Most folks never thought that a gang on horseback could rob a fast-moving train, but they hadn't reckoned with the guile and cunning of the criminal mind. Some had put obstacles across the track and one gang had rerouted the line, which caused the train to stop when it was derailed. Some had dropped from bridges as the train passed underneath, while yet other gangs boarded the train, appearing as ordinary passengers spread out through the carriages, only to come together at a prearranged time and rob the train. Larkin's best friend, Slim Johnson had refused to open up a secure part of a train that housed a strongbox and was shot through both eyes by the gang leader.

Larkin had learned to be suspicious of every passenger boarding his train. When his train stopped at Brunswick and he saw the marshal arrive at the station escorting a man, he felt the warning signs of trouble. He was remembering his trip to Tin Mountain last fall when a prisoner was being escorted by two guards who, though heavily armed hadn't been able to stop a gang boarding the train at a water stop. The gang killed the guards and two passengers died after being caught in the crossfire.

Larkin was fifty-two years old, and his liking for food was evident in his rotund frame and bloated cheeks. His cap hid his almost completely bald head. He had been pleased when a telegraph wire had informed him that a very special party would be boarding the train at Ewshot Junction. It would give him the opportunity to make a good impression and perhaps help him to gain a promotion. The train was already almost full and he had hurriedly moved some passengers and put a 'reserved' notice on the seats that would be occupied by the special party, who were due to board the train at the next stop.

Larkin had met Marshal Stockman once before when they had clashed over something trivial and the marshal had embarrassed him in front of the passengers by calling him an old woman. He was pleased when the marshal told him that the man was a personal friend of his and he would be travelling alone. The man was wearing an eye-patch; he'd obviously been in some sort of an accident or perhaps suffered an injury in the line of duty if he was a lawman.

As the marshal was preparing to leave the train after seeing him to his seat, Grainger shook his hand and thanked him for all he'd done for him, which included saving his life, not just from the mob, but from an official hanging if he had been put on trial. He had seen it in the marshal's eyes that he viewed him as some poor wretch who had been punished enough. The marshal had pitied him, but at least he was alive and he had a future with Emma. Nothing would stop that happening.

Marshal Stockman waited until the train carrying Leo Grainger disappeared behind a cloud of hissing steam. He'd never ridden on a train, but had promised his wife that they would go on one for their next vacation. He had made some brave decisions during his life and he was hoping that his decision to release Leo Grainger had been the right thing to do. It was five days since the mob had tried to hang Grainger from the support outside the saloon. He still didn't know whether Grainger had killed Jacko, but he would tell the townsfolk that Grainger had been transferred to another district for his own protection. He would have to think of some other excuse to tell the federal marshal who had taken Grainger into custody. Stockman just hoped that Grainger's fortunes would change for the better, but Leo Grainger's misery was set to continue.

★ ★ ★

Larkin adjusted his tie and brushed his hands down the front of his uniform as the train came to a stop at Ewshot Junction. He'd reread the telegram's instructions concerning his important passengers for the third time. He'd met Stanmore Poulson before and was glad that he wouldn't be with his family because Poulson was one of the few men that he had taken an instant dislike to. Although in some ways he might have had reasons to be grateful to Poulson, because he had ordered Larkin's predecessor to be sacked for some trivial matter.

Larkin told the city dude, who had escorted the family on to the train, that he had received the telegram and he would make sure that the Poulson family would be well looked after.

As the family were led to their seats Elizabeth Poulson told her two daughters not to sit down until the seats had been covered with some clean materials. Larkin hurried away and soon returned with rugs, which he placed across the seats. Elizabeth Poulson didn't offer her thanks, but reminded Larkin that her husband was the President of the railway company. She also reminded him in a loud voice that Poulson Bridge, which they would be crossing later, was named in honour of her husband and made it clear that she would be informing her husband about her trip. Larkin groaned inwardly when she told him that she had been most unimpressed during her outward journey, and was quite certain that the guard on that trip would be looking for new employment. Larkin intended to make sure that Elizabeth Poulson would have no reason to make a complaint against him to her husband. He stayed close to them until he was satisfied that the Poulson family were well settled in before he moved away and stopped to chinwag to an old acquaintance at the end of the carriage.

He had started to relax and had stopped his furtive glances towards where the Poulson family were seated, but reeled around when he heard the terrifying screams. His thoughts turned to a few months ago when some dumbass had brought a snake on to the train and it had crawled out of its basket. These screams were worse and became deafening as he hurried towards them and his anxiety levels rose when he saw that they were coming from his special passengers. The loudest screeching was from the children, but Elizabeth Poulson almost matched her daughters. All three were pointing to Grainger who was looking out of the window, still trying to clear his head having just woken up. Larkin couldn't get any sense out of the screaming females, who just kept pointing, so he went over to Grainger intending to demand to know what he had done to cause such upset. It wouldn't be the first time that he'd come across some sick minded cowboy who had exposed himself, but when Grainger turned to face him, he needed no further explanation. The eye patch that he'd worn when he boarded the train was on the floor. It must have fallen off or perhaps he had removed it, and the sight of the gaping hole and surrounding damage almost had Larkin retching.

'You'd better come with me, mister, and don't look back towards the ladies. And put that patch back on,' Larkin ordered, addressing him like a naughty schoolboy.

Grainger dutifully followed Larkin, figuring he didn't have much choice. The screaming had stopped, but he could still hear the girls sobbing as he reached the small section at the end of the carriage. He was glad when Larkin closed the dividing door.

Larkin had never had to deal with anything like this. His main priority was not the hurt feelings of this wretched man, but pacifying Mrs Elizabeth Poulson. He told Grainger to stay where he was until they could find somewhere else for him to sit where he wasn't likely to upset any of the other travellers.

When Larkin returned after his discussions with an irate Mrs Poulson, who had made it clear that his future position was in grave danger, he told Grainger that he would have to stay in the cramped section of the train for now. He promised Grainger a good seat, further down the train but well away from the Poulson family, when someone left the train at the next stop.

★　★　★

Grainger eventually grew tired of standing and viewing the rolling scene that remained unchanged mile after mile. His legs had become stiff and the shin where the bullet had ripped into the bone was throbbing. He eased himself down on to the floor of the cramped section of the train where he had been confined, feeling that it was less comfortable than the cell he had been in that very morning. He eventually drifted off to sleep, helped by the rocking motion of the train. He hadn't realized that the train would come to a halt until he was shaken awake by Larkin, who told him that they had stopped to take on board some water from a tank near the track. He suggested that Grainger get off the train and stretch his legs and Grainger was pleased when Larkin told him that they would soon be at the next station, when he would find him a comfortable seat.

Grainger had been raised in the lush valleys and surrounding hills near Bordon Valley and had taken a different route on his journey to find his brother. He had never experienced such barren land as that which he could now see. It was mostly rocky with just the odd patch of greenery, and clumps of small trees. When he spotted the assortment of rusty metal which included small sections of track he figured that the railway workers might have used this spot as a base.

He could see the start of a mountain range in the distance and wondered what name it went by and whether it was the same one he had ridden close to some weeks ago. There was a tiny wooden hut that had some slats missing and others that were thin and crumbling pieces of softwood. The fading letters on door indicated that it was a latrine and Grainger hobbled towards it. Once inside he wished he had waited until the next stop. The smell of dried faeces hit his nostrils and the sound of buzzing flies filled the small wooden hut. Maybe the rotten carcass of a small animal that he didn't recognize might have been the attraction for flies as they competed with the cluster of white maggots. He hurriedly pulled up his pants when he heard the sound of the train's whistle and the hiss of steam that meant the train was ready to move on. He needn't have hurried because the train was already gathering speed when he emerged from the hut. He stumbled onto the stony ground beside the track as he tried to run alongside it, hoping to climb aboard.

The train hadn't taken on any water and Larkin had fulfilled Elizabeth Poulson's demand that Grainger be removed from the train. Grainger hadn't seen her smug expression as her section of the train passed him or Larkin's guilt-ridden face as he peered out of the window and saw the forlorn figure whom he had almost certainly doomed to his death and a feast for the buzzards. Larkin could only hope that God would forgive him being a party to the poor soul's demise.

Grainger struggled to get up. By the time he managed it the last carriage had passed him. He hobbled to a small platform on which was a wooden bench. He felt desperate and feared that the unexpected action by the kindly marshal who had released him would be wasted. All his plans for a future had been destroyed by the screams of that hysterical woman and her children. He felt the taste of salt in his mouth and realized that his tears had trickled down on to his lips. He lay on the bench and sobbed. He had no thought of survival, he just wanted to drift into a sleep and never wake up.

★ ★ ★

The heat of the sun sent him into a state of delirium, causing thoughts and images to flash though his mind. He pictured his ma welcoming him on his return from the small white wooden clapboard school and his trips to church every Sunday. He recalled his pa admonishing him for not fighting Donny Stokes who had bullied him, and asking him why he couldn't be like his brother.

His recollection of his first conversation with Emma Linton at a barn dance was interrupted when he realized that he was not alone. The moving shadow made him look to the sky and he saw the buzzards circling above. Perhaps it was his memories of Emma or the fear of the buzzards pecking at his dying flesh that made him stagger to his feet, ready to move on. He remembered seeing a water pump and hobbled towards it. His prayers were answered when he pulled the handle and water spluttered out on to the ground. The water was warm, but still welcome as he drank his fill, then splashed it over himself. He remembered that he had brought a water bottle that had been given to him by the marshal; he retrieved it from near the bench and filled it to the brim. He felt in a better mood now, and less despondent, although he knew that his plight was still desperate because of his injured leg and the rough terrain. He would follow the railway line for a while, hoping that he might see another train coming towards him, because he knew that there was only one train a week that was home-ward bound. He didn't know how he would stop the train, but perhaps he would be seen by a passenger who would raise the alarm.

By the time the light was fading his feet were blistered and his mouth was parched despite several stops to take small sips from the water bottle, not knowing how long the meagre supply would have to last him. He hadn't seen a train or any signs of life, apart from the buzzards that had perched on a rock close to him, but they had flown away when he hurled small stones at them. He expected them to be back when daylight came. By then he might not have the strength to hurl even a small stone and would have to use his gun. He tried to select the best spot to bed down for the night, but there didn't seem much choice. He settled in amongst a small group of rocks not far from the track. Perhaps it was his mind playing tricks when he heard the hiss of a snake before he had drifted into a deep sleep.

★ ★ ★

It was barely light when Grainger woke. He felt stiffness in his neck and his injured leg was throbbing again. When he sat up and pulled up the leg of his pants he wasn't surprised to see the open wound. Perhaps it was the stumble he had taken in running for the train, or he might have disturbed it in the night during his restless attempts to find a comfortable position on the mostly hard ground where he had chosen to bed down. A sip of his dwindling supply of water had no effect on his parched mouth, but he resisted the temptation to take another. He pulled down the leg of his pants to cover the wound and managed to stagger to his feet, but cried out in pain.

The sky was clear, but still darkened and he hoped it was too early for the buzzards, but he had heard some scurrying sounds amongst the rocks. Marshal Stockman had returned his Colt .45 so at least there was a chance of him killing a small animal if he was quick enough, but for the moment his hunger wasn't great enough to contemplate tearing into raw flesh, because he had no means of cooking anything he might kill.

Come mid-morning he had made slow progress, hampered by his injured leg. The railway track still disappeared into the distance and the mountain range started to seem a more tempting route because he could see hillocks and woodland areas not too far away.

* * *

When the sun was high in the sky and he had grown weary of wishfully thinking that a train might appear he stopped for a sip of water and decided he would head in the direction of the trees. It was a decision that would have him collapsing to the ground in despair less than half an hour later when he turned in the direction of the noise and saw a train moving at slow speed in the direction of Brunswick.

It had taken all his resolve to stagger from the ground where he had stayed after he'd seen the train. His progress was slow and the light was fading by the time he reached a group of small trees. He pulled a leaf from the nearest branch and began chewing it without bothering to test whether it was edible. He discovered that it had a slight minty taste which was bearable, and even though the centre had a bitter taste he still swallowed it. Satisfied that they would stem his hunger he gathered leaves from the nearest trees and staggered to the small group of rocks clutching the leaves in both hands. He chose the smoothest-faced rock, rested his back against it, then prepared to munch into the leaves. Some tasted bitter and he spat them into the ground, but he was soon regretting not bringing more to where he planned to bed down. The large swig from the water bottle helped remove the after-taste of the leaves, then he tried to find a comfortable spot on a soft sandy section of the ground. He soon drifted into a sleep and this time he had no nightmares to contend with, at least not while he was slumbering.

★ ★ ★

Passing his tongue over his dry lips he felt the urge to vomit, and then a wave of griping pains in his stomach had him wincing in agony. He forced open his eyelids and surveyed the clear blue sky and the bright sun, thinking that it was the sun that had awakened him. He raised his body to sit up and reached down to gently test the area of his injured leg. He jolted in surprise when he saw movement inside the leg of his pants. He'd slept with his gunbelt still fastened to his waist and he drew his pistol, not knowing whether it was a large insect, small animal or snake that had been ferreting around his bloodied leg. He jumped up to a standing position, forgetting about his injury, then shook the leg of his pants, waiting for whatever it was to appear, but it must have scurried away.

The pistol was still in his hand when he heard a scraping sound to his right. He whirled around and saw a rat burrowing into the soft sand. That must have been what had crawled inside his pants; he decided it would be better to kill it in case he chose to camp in this spot until he was stronger. He slowly raised his pistol to take aim, closing his left eye intending to line up the target, but he could see nothing. He had forgotten that he no longer had a right eye. He readjusted his pistol's line of fire, cocked it, ready to pull the trigger, but the rat had hurried away on hearing the click of the pistol's hammer.

'Damn,' he cursed, but he was soon to use stronger words when he reached for the water bottle and discovered that most of its content had spilled into the sand because he had not secured the top properly. He lifted the bottle to his lips and finished the last dregs of water, but it was wasted when he spewed the greenish vomit into the sand. He would forget his plans to sample another batch of leaves, fearing that he might have actually poisoned himself.

He still felt nausea and weakness as he prepared to continue his trek, but at least the vomiting had stopped and he wiped the back of his hand across his mouth to remove the remnants of it. He had slept soundly, but when he prepared to walk on he felt drained and unsteady. Grainger emerged from the trees believing that it was likely that he would die today unless he found some water. He surveyed the scene in front of him and put his hand to his head. He was wondering whether he had a fever or an infection, but his skin felt normal to his touch. Perhaps it wasn't a mirage, but the effects of the leaves, or he was just imagining what he thought he could see. He'd heard tales of men having hallucinations after they had smoked the leaves of certain trees. Now he prayed to God that the house he could see in the distance was real. He hoped he would have the strength to reach it.

11

Josie Tolman was struggling to catch the rooster which was destined for her dinner plate when she spotted the man staggering towards her. He looked too old to be of any use to her, but she wondered how he could be so far off the trail and yet be travelling on foot. Her back was aching and she felt sweaty. She decided to give the rooster a stay of execution, pulled a neckerchief from her pocket and used it to wipe the beads of sweat from her brow.

Josie was thirty-six years old, dark-haired and brown-eyed. Some would say she was attractive in a womanly way that most men like, but she could not be described as pretty. The plump cheeks were reddened rather than tanned and her lips were full. She pouted them on the rare occasions when she didn't have a cigarette between them. She reached for the shotgun that was propped against the door of the shed and walked towards the man, who now seemed on the point of collapse.

The man raised his hand as she approached and turned his face to the side. His lips were dry and blistered and his voice was weak as he said in a whisper, 'Help me.'

Josie lowered the rifle as she realized that the man was no threat to anyone, even though he was only young and not the old man that his gait had suggested. He kept his face away from her, but when she went to his side to help him walk towards her house she saw why. Her face showed her shock, but she resisted asking him what had happened to him. She draped his arm over her shoulder, but he held on to the empty water bottle when she tried to take it from his hand. His expression was wild and distrusting even though he had begged her to help him. She managed to calm him and continued on their slow walk towards the double-fronted cabin that had once been her husband's pride and joy, but was now showing the early signs of neglect.

The mangy-looking dog that had been asleep on the porch looked at Grainger, but lowered its head back between its paws, its cheeks puffing as though signalling that he was neglected or plain fed up. Josie carefully eased Grainger back towards the rocking-chair that was in a shaded spot on the porch, and he slumped in to it with a thud.

'Gently does it, mister. You look all in. Just lie back there and I'll bring you some of my home-made lemonade. My husband has a stock of funny plants and herbs and things which he taught me how to use, but I've done a bit of experimenting and added a thing or two. My lemonade's got more of a kick in it than that watery beer you boys drink.'

Grainger muttered a weary, 'Thank, you ma'am,' lay back and closed his eyes, but he had heard her laugh and say, 'Josie's the name, and I ain't old enough or respectable enough to be called a ma'am.'

Grainger was asleep when Josie returned with a drink and she decided to leave him be, but he moved and muttered some words, as if he was having a nightmare or was delirious. Josie knelt by his side and calmed him with soothing words, then offered the cup of cool lemonade to his lips. She told him to sip it, but he took it from her, gulped it down, then handed the empty cup back as he thanked her.

'You rest there awhile, and then you can come inside and I'll prepare some food for us. I had something special in mind until that rooster over there had other ideas, but he won't be so cocky tomorrow.' The rooster was at the bottom of the porch steps and he tilted his head on one side as though he was listening to her.

Grainger was thinking that perhaps his luck really had changed. Shortly before he'd spotted the woman he had

131

been on the point of lying down to die, because the house he was walking towards hadn't seemed to be getting any closer. It was only the memory of Emma and the future they could have together that had given him the resolve to carry on. He wondered where the woman's husband was and whether there would be a chance of stealing a horse, but his curiosity was soon to be solved when the woman returned and told him that his food was ready.

'It's been a while since I cooked for anyone else, but I think you'd probably eat just about anything and there's some coffee brewing.'

Josie offered to help him up from the seat, but he declined, feeling stronger already. He was directed to a seat near the table that was covered in a spotless red-and-white check tablecloth. A candle was burning and as it flickered he surveyed the room that was quite dark because the heavy wooden shutters had been closed.

Grainger felt uncomfortable but

grateful as he waded through the large plate of beans in between bites on the fresh bread. The reason for his discomfort was that the woman who had introduced herself as Josie was sitting opposite and seemed to be studying him as she puffed away on the cigarette that she'd rolled. He guessed she was waiting for him to speak. When he didn't she asked where he was heading and before he replied she asked about his 'injuries'. He lied and told her that he had been set on by a gang and his horse had been stolen while he was heading back to Bordon Valley.

'I've been there, used to work in a saloon, and I've been back a few times with my husband. We used to follow the railway track until we saw the sign to the Crookham River Bridge, then we'd head for there and cross the bridge. You'll never make it on foot because it used to take us best part of two days.'

'Maybe I could stop the train if one came by,' he suggested without really believing it was possible.

'I have an idea that might help both of us,' Josie suggested. Grainger remembered similar words being used by Bradley, but whatever Josie had in mind he was certain that it wasn't a bank robbery.

'Don't look so worried, Lee.'

Grainger had told her his name was Leo but he didn't bother correcting her and she continued to explain her idea.

'I've got a couple of horses in the corral out at the back and there's quite a lot of jobs need doing around here that are really a man's work. Perhaps when you're feeling strong enough you could help me out and you can take one of the horses.'

The suggestion was welcome news to Grainger. He was thinking that if he worked hard then it might only be a matter of days before he could head home to Emma. So he readily accepted Josie's offer and told her that he would be ready to start work in the morning.

Josie insisted that he had her bed that night because he needed to get his strength back. She supplied him with a nightshirt that had belonged to her husband who, she had revealed, had just upped and gone some months earlier. When Josie wasn't inhaling smoke from her cigarette she would talk and Grainger had heard her life story before at last he managed to get away to the peace of the small bedroom. Josie had arranged a makeshift bed on the floor of the only other room in the small cabin and said that she planned to do some sewing before she turned in, even though she hated doing it.

★　★　★

Grainger had slept soundly and when he woke the welcome smell of cooking drifted in to his room. He eased himself off the bed and although there was still stiffness in his body he felt refreshed and better than he had for some time. He dressed quickly in the clothes that Josie had given him and figured that Josie's husband must have been about his

135

height. They felt better than the torn and dusty ones that she had taken away to wash.

Josie greeted him with a cheery smile. She was wearing a bright-red blouse and only the bottom button was fastened. She had let her hair down so that it rested on her shoulders and as he sat down at the table he detected that the smell of perfume was competing with the smell of eggs and beans that Josie had set before him. She smiled when he focused on her unbuttoned blouse, not knowing that his thoughts were elsewhere.

After breakfast Josie invited Grainger to walk around outside as she identified the various jobs that she would like him to do. Then she led him to the small shed, which contained a fine collection of tools. She left it to him to decide in what order he would tackle the jobs, so he started with repairing the broken corral fence. Josie had told him the sandy bay was her horse, but he could take his pick from the sorrel and the roan. He wondered whether both the mares were with foal, or perhaps they just hadn't been exercised in a long time. Josie joked that he could only have the horse if his work was up to standard, and that included another little job she had in mind for him. She smiled and did an exaggerated wiggle of her hips as she walked away. She was still smiling coyly when she turned around and looked his way, but he'd headed towards the barn to pick up some wood and she was disappointed.

★   ★   ★

The sun was at its hottest before Grainger heeded Josie's suggestion to stop work and take a rest. Josie had prepared some sandwiches and a cool drink which she said was the last of her husband's home-brewed beer. Grainger wondered why her husband had left her alone, but his decision not to ask her didn't matter because she insisted on telling him. It seemed that Jethro

Tolman had been a cold man, not fond of showing his affections towards his wife, but he had been intensely jealous and had not taken kindly to Josie paying attention to the various men who had passed their way.

Josie's parting words to Grainger before he returned to his work were that her husband didn't understand that she had her needs just like any red-blooded cowboy.

★　★　★

It was still light and Grainger had expected to work for another few hours when Josie shouted from the porch way that dinner was ready. A tired Grainger downed tools and headed towards the cabin. He was pleased with the work he'd done because it wasn't something he had ever enjoyed doing and now he was able to strike three jobs off Josie's list. Grainger figured that it would take him no more than another couple of days to finish the work, then he could be on his way home and would soon be telling Emma about his true feelings. There would be no more holding back. He knew that she liked him, but he had risked losing her just because he was too reserved. The new Grainger was stronger. He had been through hell, but now he could see some good coming from it, even though there might still be some unfinished business.

During dinner Josie told Grainger about her early life and how she'd met her husband while working in a saloon in Savannah Plains. She'd agreed to marry him just three weeks after their first meeting. He had told her about the wonderful place he'd inherited from his pa. It had seemed idyllic and it was, for someone who liked to live the life of a recluse.

By the time they'd finished eating Josie's stew and beans and they had both drunk some more of Josie's home-made lemonade she had become giggly, but the meal had made Grainger drowsy. After he'd been yawning at regular intervals for some time she suggested he should think about going to bed. Josie insisted that Grainger should again sleep in the only bed in the house, because he needed to be strong for another heavy day's work in the morning. Grainger agreed that he was tired; he bid her goodnight and left her filling up another glass with lemonade.

He decided against wearing the nightshirt that Josie had provided him with because the tiny bedroom felt warm. Within a few minutes of pulling the bed sheet over his naked body he was asleep.

Grainger's first thoughts when he felt the softness of a woman's naked body against his back was that he was dreaming, and he didn't move when the hands explored his manhood. It was the familiar smell of Josie's perfume that made his body stiffen before he turned to face the smiling Josie, who pressed herself against him.

'You had me worried for a moment,

cowboy. I thought I'd lost my touch or you didn't find me attractive or maybe thought I was just too old for you.'

Grainger was about to speak when her lips met his, then he felt her tongue inside his mouth, which was something that he'd never experienced before. He wanted to push her away, but knew that she would be offended. She was behaving like a common saloon girl and he felt that he was betraying Emma, but Josie rubbed herself against him and his thoughts of Emma and any feeling of guilt momentarily disappeared. Josie directed him on to his back, then straddled him and groaned as she felt his arousal. She then cried out as he entered her. She guided his hands to her breasts as she moved up and down in a gentle rhythm, then her movements became frantic and her sighing and moaning were new to him. He felt her body shudder as she cried out, then kissed his face all over before he felt her gasping hot breath in his ear.

Josie lifted herself off him and rolled

on to her back beside him. She smiled as she said, 'I've a feeling that was your first time, cowboy, but I'm sure not complaining, because I haven't had anything inside me for nigh on a month and it was nothing special the last time. That good-for-nothing husband of mine couldn't give me the child I wanted and maybe you just have. He said I was too old, but my ma was forty-four when she had me and I reckon I'm just as fertile as my ma was.'

Grainger didn't reply; his emotions were a confused mixture. Josie wasn't confused at all as she cuddled up to him; she was determined that she wouldn't let him leave her. He could be happy here and avoid the rejection he would face by almost every other woman he would meet apart from a saloon girl willing to take his money and make love to him in the darkness while trying to block out the memory of his face. Grainger was breathing heavily and for a short while he felt relaxed, but the satisfied feeling slowly left him and it was replaced by guilt. The guilt was joined by revulsion when Josie whispered a string of crude suggestions in his ear and began rubbing herself against him, inviting him to come on top of her.

12

Emma Linton waved to her pa as he flicked the whip and the carriage moved away. John Linton said he would pick her up in an hour when he'd had the sorrel's shoes replaced at the black-smiths. It was the first time that Emma had been into Bordon since Donny Stokes's funeral, except for her Sunday visits to the church. She didn't know why some of the older womenfolk had glared at her, because she wasn't to blame for Donny's death. She wouldn't deny that she'd had her feelings for Donny, and for some of the other young men, including those she'd grown up with, but she was confused and frightened. Her pa had told that no man could be trusted. They would tell her lies and they would be after only one thing. She had never even kissed a boy, but she knew what her pa meant, and some of her friends had told her things that had made her blush. Those funny feelings that she'd started getting as a young girl were much stronger now. When she'd told her pa that she wasn't a girl any more he had shown a temper she'd never seen before and accused her of being just like her mother. He'd calmed down later and explained that he only wanted to protect her, but he'd only made her feel unhappy. She had liked Donny Stokes and she liked the Grainger brothers, but it wasn't true to say that she had flirted with them all and caused trouble between them. Following Donny's killing she had wanted to leave town and go and live with her favourite Aunt Muriel in Colbray Falls, but her pa had shown his temper again and refused to let her go.

The man coming out of the general store tipped his hat and gave her a smile. As was her nature she returned it, just as Hilda Monkton, the mayor's wife was approaching. She gave Emma a cold, disapproving look. Emma was thinking that she might have to defy her pa soon and leave home, because no self-respecting man would want to come calling while folks were still whispering behind her back. It just wasn't fair.

Norman Douglas had run the general store on his own ever since his wife Julia had died three years ago after being bitten by a snake while they were picnicking. Some said that her face had ballooned to three times its size. Norman had tried to suck out the poison, but Julia was dead within minutes. Doc Bennett had said it was likely a heart attack and she wouldn't have suffered, but Norman could still remember his wife screaming and recall the agony on her face when he lay awake some nights. Norman was a churchgoing man and believed that everything happened for a purpose, which was why he continued to be the same happy-go-lucky person he'd been before Julia died. He had just finished serving a young cowboy with his first pistol when Emma walked into the store, carrying a small shopping-basket.

'Now here's just about the prettiest girl that ever walked into my store since the day I opened too many years ago to remember.'

The young cowboy smiled at Emma as he passed and stepped into the street, thinking that the old storekeeper wasn't exaggerating. He hadn't seen the girl before, but he would be remembering those pale-blue eyes and petite little face with a slightly turned-up nose. Most of all he would be remembering that shapely body, which was shown off by that snug-fitting ruby-welvet dress.

'Good to see you, Miss Linton. Your pa was in here only yesterday, picking up your supplies. So what brings you here today?'

Emma felt all the better for the friendly welcome and explained about her pa needing to take the horse to the blacksmith. She was just going to have a look around the store to see if there were any nice lace items, or perhaps a pretty scarf.

Emma felt relaxed as she wandered around the store viewing the various items. In the end she purchased a small purse with a floral pattern and a scarf to match. Douglas often joked with her in a fatherly way and was never suggestive, like some older men were, forgetting that they were old enough to be her pa and in some cases, even grandpa.

'You'll break someone's heart one day, Miss Linton, but it won't be your fault.'

She gave him a sweet smile and thanked him as he held open the door. She stepped out on to the sidewalk to wait for her pa, only to be greeted by another man who usually made her feel at ease. It was Marshal Stephens and he surprised her when he said that he needed to warn her about something; however she needn't worry.

'Old Josh Morrison swears that when his stagecoach stopped to water the horses at Coogan's Point he saw Scott

Grainger and another man leaving and heading this way.'

'Thank you kindly for your concern, Marshal, but I have no reason to fear Scott Grainger. Despite what folks say, I don't believe he had anything to do with Donny Stokes's killing.'

Marshal Stephens was thinking that Grainger would be a fool to come back to town and face a certain hanging, but some men did daft things for a pretty face and they didn't come any prettier than Emma Linton. He was also thinking that Emma Linton wouldn't be the first woman who couldn't see any wrong in a man whom most other folks knew was evil. He didn't think Scott Grainger was exactly evil, but he felt certain that he was capable of killing a man.

Marshal Stephens said that he just thought she should know, told her again not to worry, tipped his hat and made his way across Main Street to his office, leaving Emma with her troubled thoughts. She wondered whether she should tell her pa about Scott. Of all the men who had shown interest in her it was Scott whom her pa disapproved of most. Scott was about the most handsome man she had ever seen, but everyone knew that he had a liking for saloon girls. Emma suspected that her mother had run away with Mr Snyder, the bank manager, just last year because he was a handsome-looking man with lots of charm. She loved her pa dearly, but he was the ugliest man in town with an oversized nose, ears to match and eyes that were half-covered by his droopy eyelids. Emma smiled as she remembered that when she was first attracting the attention of the young boys her mother had told Emma that it's not what's in a man's face and body that counts, but what's in his heart. It seems her ma didn't practise what she preached.

Emma saw the cloud of dust that was caused by her pa driving the carriage towards her. She had never forgotten her odd sense of relief when she had heard that Leo Grainger had told the marshal that his brother Scott had confessed to killing Donny Stokes. The killing had happened on the same day that her pa had galloped away from their home saying that he was going to tell Donny Stokes to stay clear of Emma or he would kill him.

13

Scott Grainger pointed towards the rundown cabin that had belonged to a family before his pa bought their land and they moved on. His pa had planned to use the land, but he never did and no one ever came out this way. He told Mackenzie that was where they could stay until they had done the bank job.

Mackenzie had been in worse-looking places than the rundown cabin, so he didn't comment as they approached what would be their home for at least a couple of days.

'So who is this woman you've come to see?' Mackenzie asked when they had finished their grub and had settled down on their matching single beds. Mackenzie took a deep puff on his cheroot and blew a cloud of smoke above him while he waited for an answer. Grainger's thoughts had been elsewhere and his reply was delivered in a matter-of-fact manner. He wasn't really wanting to discuss it.

'She's just a girl I grew up with. She was more like a sister until she started to fill out, and I guess I've missed her more than I thought I would.'

'How old are you, Grainger?'

'Twenty-five come next month.'

'Jesus, that's no age to be thinking of being shackled to a nagging woman who'll likely lose her looks after she's had a few babies. She'll let herself go and you'll be thinking of me and the new gang I'll set up, bedding a different woman every time we felt horny. No strings and no nagging.'

'I've had my share of women, and if you saw Emma Linton you'd understand why I'm hoping she'll come away with me. The thing I didn't tell you, Mack, is that I killed a man over her and that's why that bounty hunter came after me and that's why I'll need to stay away from town until the actual robbery in case someone sees me and tells the marshal.'

'Spare me the hearts-and-roses shit. You'll be telling me that you can't live without her next. No woman's worth risking a hanging for.'

'I don't expect you to understand, buddy, but she is a bit special.'

'So what's she like, this woman? I know you like them busty, so I guess she must have a fine pair of titties.' Mackenzie laughed.

Grainger smiled and replied, 'She's not your sort of woman, Mack. In fact you could best describe her as a lady.'

Mackenzie frowned. 'A lady, you say. Take it from me there ain't any such thing as a lady. I've been with a few church-going married women who were all airs and graces and acted proper prudish. You know, the sort who look as though butter wouldn't melt in their mouths until they were lying on their backs. Then they weren't any different from the commonest saloon girl.'

'Emma's different,' Grainger replied.

'You'll be telling me next that she's saving herself for you. I never had you down as a dumb-ass, Grainger, but I bet you fifty bucks from the bank money that she's been keeping someone happy while you've been away.'

Grainger didn't answer for some moments as he dwelled on what Mackenzie had said, then told him that he couldn't take his money.

Mackenzie hadn't mentioned the encounter with his brother before they were interrupted by the federal marshal, but Grainger wasn't surprised that he brought the subject up as they sipped some of the whiskey they'd bought when they'd stopped at Coogan's Point to buy some grub.

'So, what do you figure that freak who Bradley brought in to the camp was up to, claiming that you were his brother?'

'He had to have been a bounty hunter like they figured in Brunswick,' Grainger replied.

'Perhaps he'd hoped to get an opportunity to plug you and maybe the rest of us and hadn't reckoned on

Bradley covering him with his gun. He just tried to bluff his way when he saw you. The son of a bitch got what was coming to him.'

'I guess he did,' replied Grainger, wondering what he was going to tell his pa when he met him.

14

Leo Grainger had covered just a hundred yards when he pulled up Josie's sandy bay and looked back towards Josie's homestead. He'd washed his body under the water pump before he'd saddled Josie's horse, but he could still smell Josie on him and he felt dirty. She'd promised him the pick of the other two horses, but on closer inspection neither looked up to carrying him on the long ride to Bordon Valley.

He remembered what Josie had said about the route she had taken with her husband and he turned his mount towards the narrow trail that led down to the railtrack. Had it not been for that hysterical snooty woman he would have been home by now, but if his plans worked out he would spend the rest of his life with Emma, so a few days' delay wouldn't make much difference. Marshal

Stockman had told him not to worry about being listed as a wanted man because he would take care of things, but there were other matters that he might have to take care of himself.

By the time the light faded the trip had taken longer than he had expected. He stopped when he saw the signpost to the Crookham River Bridge that Josie had mentioned. If all went well he would be home tomorrow and he could start fulfilling his hopes and dreams. As he bedded down for the night he wondered what had become of his brother. He hadn't been surprised to discover that he was a member of a gang because Scott had always courted excitement and danger.

Grainger had left Josie lying on her back in the bed where he'd had his first experience with a woman and he remembered the pleasure he had felt. She'd told him that she wanted him to stay and if he insisted on leaving then she would follow him to Bordon Valley. She'd said that she fell in love easily and that she loved him and she needed him.

Grainger had been dozing since the sound of the fast-flowing river and the early-morning birds had woken him. When he heard a gruff voice say, 'If this ugly bastard has stolen Josie's horse then we'll hang him from that tree', he thought he was dreaming, but he wasn't. Two men were staring down at him and both had pistols in their hands.

15

Tobias Stokes swayed as he rose from
the rocking chair on the porch of the
small cabin, which was surrounded by
rubbish and empty bottles. Stokes was
fifty-eight years old and had once been
a man who took a pride in himself and
his business, but not any more. He
picked up the half-empty whiskey bottle
and stepped off the porch, ready to
greet the rider who was approaching.
He didn't get too many visitors since
his son had been killed and his wife had
gone to live with her sister in the next
town after she'd got fed up with his
drinking. Perhaps she'd come back one
day, but he didn't care any more. Not
about his wife, his business or anything
else, except his drinking. The drinking
helped him when no one else could.
That good-for-nothing marshal had
fobbed him off with excuses about it

being a big country and believed that Scott Grainger had almost certainly settled outside his jurisdiction.

The man dismounting was John Linton, his nearest neighbour, to whom he hadn't spoken since his son's funeral. He wasn't really welcome here. If his flirty daughter, Emma, hadn't been so man mad his son would still be alive. He'd told him to stay away from her because she wasn't ever going to be the faithful sort, but his son had been smitten by her, just like Scott Grainger and all the other young, horny men who saw her. She might have tried to be a little helpless, churchgoing miss, but she knew she drove men crazy and she enjoyed it.

'What do you want, Linton? Have you come to invite me to your whore of a daughter's wedding because she's gotten a swollen belly? I don't suppose she knows who the father is.'

John Linton sighed, but managed to control his anger as he looked at the pathetic man in front of him.

'There's no call for that, Tobias. I have always been proud of my daughter and you bad-mouthing her won't bring back your son whose death had nothing to do with her. I've come here because there is something you might want to know about.'

Stokes put the whiskey bottle he'd been holding to his lips, took a long swig from it, and then swayed once again as he struggled to find the words.

'You've got nothing that I would want to know about. Now get off my land.'

John Linton had thought long and hard about coming out to see his neighbour, but he wasn't prepared to take any more abusive and totally ill-founded comments about his sweet daughter.

'Suit yourself, you bitter son of a bitch. I felt sorry for you like other folks do, but you are wallowing in self-pity. I came to tell you about Scott Grainger.'

Tobias Stokes's face turned to fury at the mere mention of the name, but his attitude changed.

'Wait. I shouldn't have said those things, but I still think my son died because he was sweet on your daughter, because nothing else makes sense. What did you want to tell me about Grainger?'

'He's back and in hiding somewhere. Don't ask me how I know. I thought you might want to tell Marshal Stephens.'

Stokes tried to clear his brain. It seemed that his prayers had been answered and he wouldn't be going to any marshal. Soon his son would be able to lie in peace and his own torment would be over. He wondered how Seth Grainger would take the news that his son had been gunned down in cold blood.

As Linton turned his horse to ride off he had a warning for Stokes, but he was confident that it probably wouldn't be heeded. 'Don't do anything stupid, Tobias, and end up at the end of a rope. You can't bring your son back.'

Linton was hoping that by telling Tobias Stokes about Grainger's return he might have saved his daughter future grief, because he suspected that she still had strong feelings for Scott Grainger, a man whom he disliked intensely. Until he'd killed Donny Stokes he had never done anything really bad as far as folks knew, but he had a wild streak in him and was too quick to use his fists. He had been no stranger to the cells in town after many a barroom brawl. Scott Grainger and his brother Leo were like chalk and cheese.

Toad Stokes walked out on to the porch, yawned and stretched as his pa climbed the steps and joined him on the porch after he'd watched Linton ride off.

'Who was that, Pa?' Toad asked as he hitched his pants up and scratched between his legs.

'It was John Linton and he came to tell me that your brother's killer has returned. So you and me are going to find the bastard and save the town the trouble of a trial and a hanging. We could have our own private lynching, but we'll just gun him down like he did Donny.'

Toad Stokes looked uncomfortable and did some more scratching as his pa continued to talk about revenge and justice. Toad had hoped that Scott Grainger was already dead, or at least would never set foot in these parts ever again.

'This is your chance to make amends for not being here for your brother's funeral,' Tobias said, his face flushed with the anticipation of long-sought revenge.

'Perhaps we should just tell Marshal Stephens, then we can watch Scott hang along with all the other folks. Wouldn't that be best, Pa?' Toad suggested, hoping his pa would calm down and see some sense.

Tobias Stokes snarled back at his son. 'No, it wouldn't. Don't you go all chicken-livered on me, because if you don't help me get rid of Scott Grainger then you can get your fat ass out of here now and never come back. Perhaps your ma was giving it to some no-good cowboy while I was flogging away and you're not my son after all.'

Toad Stokes was short, and his belt was on its last notch on account of his overhanging belly. His hair was already receding and his red cheeks were puffed out, giving the impression he was blowing up a balloon. Nature hadn't been kind to Todd Stokes and some of the boys had started calling him Toad and it had stuck, but he didn't seem to mind that.

'What do you mean, Pa?' Toad asked with the puzzled look that he frequently had.

'You ain't that dumb. Now no more talk of the marshal.'

Tobias Stokes made an instant decision and threw the whiskey bottle into the dust having decided that he wouldn't be needing to drown his sorrow in whiskey once his son's killer was dead.

Toad had been pondering over his plight and he decided that he would leave his crazy pa. He had argued with his brother on the day he died and told him he was wasting his time sniffing after Emma Linton. The dumb-ass had taken no notice and must have taken on Scott Grainger. Toad had left town shortly after the argument and lived rough for a week before the hunger pangs in his belly made him return home. Toad liked Emma Linton because she was the only girl he'd met who smiled and talked to him when they crossed paths in town. He understood why men fought over her, but he had no intention of facing a hangman's noose to avenge his stupid brother's death.

16

Mackenzie had ridden into Bordon Valley the previous day and familiarized himself with the bank's location, He had discussed the plan again with Grainger before they left their shack that morning. It was agreed that after the robbery they would split the money equally and Mackenzie would head for the next town, which was Acker. He would wait there three days for Grainger, in case the woman he was all gooey-eyed over turned him down. If Grainger didn't show up he would ride on to Hyatt Falls and start enjoying himself.

It was mid-morning and Main Street was quiet. Norman Douglas was sweeping the dust from the sidewalk outside his store and two ladies were passing the time of day outside Chuck's Diner. The ladies said their farewells as

Mackenzie dismounted outside the bank and they both frowned at him as he handed his reins to Grainger as planned. Despite the ladies' disapproving looks there was nothing suspicious about Mackenzie as he mounted the steps and eased open the door of the bank.

Karl Bruggen who owned the Watering Hole saloon was crossing Main Street heading for the bank to deposit the previous night's takings when the sound of gunfire made him halt in his tracks. Bruggen jumped aside and fell to the ground to avoid being trampled on by Mackenzie's horse as it galloped away, startled by the sound of gunfire coming from inside the bank. Bruggen didn't bother to pick up the moneybag as he scrambled to his feet and hurried back across the street to take refuge in his saloon. Once safely inside he couldn't resist peering over the saloon doors, from where he saw a man emerge from the bank with his hands above his head. Marshal Charlie Stephens and his deputy were behind him and both had their pistols pointing at his back.

Mackenzie scanned both ways along Main Street and spotted his horse some distance away, looking as though it was waiting for someone to climb up on to its back. Scott Grainger was nowhere to be seen.

While the deputy secured Mackenzie in one of the three cells, Marshal Stephens spread the three Wanted posters on his desk. One was for a series of stagecoach robberies: the wanted man was Jack Merton, alias Malcolm Mackenzie. Another was for killing a deputy marshal in Melksham Springs and the wanted man was Malcolm Mackenzie. The most recent was for a double killing during a bank robbery and the wanted man was Malcolm Mackenzie. The artist's sketch on all three posters bore a striking resemblance to the man whom the marshal could hear complaining that he had been wrongly arrested and that he had gone to the bank to make an enquiry.

Mackenzie was still complaining

when Marshal Stephens went to his cell and told him that if he didn't stop hollering he wouldn't be getting fed later. Then he added, 'You haven't got many meals left before they hang you, Mackenzie, so you might want to bear that in mind.'

'Dream on, Marshal. They'll be burying your old bones in the ground a long time before mine. My buddy will make sure that I don't spend much time in this shithole.'

'And who would your buddy be?' the marshal asked.

Mackenzie tapped a finger against his nose to suggest that it was a secret, then said, 'I ain't no snitch turd, Marshal, but you'll meet him soon enough and he'll bring enough men with him to take care of you and your deputies. If he finds out that you've got a little wife tucked away somewhere then we might just burn your house down before we leave town.'

Marshal Stephens didn't reply as he turned and walked away, but he still heard Mackenzie's final threat of: 'Do yourself a favour, old man. Leave the cell door open when you go to do your rounds tonight and we'll never bother you again.'

17

Seth Grainger was a hard taskmaster, but a fair man. As he sat behind his large desk in the study of his ranch house he was more troubled than he had ever been in his life. The unexpected events and news he'd heard just an hour earlier still hadn't sunk in properly, but he wanted to sort out at least one of the consequences, which was why he had sent for his foreman, Jeff Friedel. Friedel had worked hard since he had taken on the job after Seth's son Scott had left. Although Grainger hadn't made any promises regarding the future he could tell by his recent conversation that Friedel expected the job to be permanent.

Seth Grainger was sixty-three years old and still a powerfully built man. The square jaw and dark, cold eyes had always made men wary of tangling with him, and he'd managed to build a sizeable ranch without making too many enemies. He'd just placed the photograph of his two boys on one side when he responded to the knock on his study door and invited the caller in.

Jeff Friedel looked pleased. It was only the second time he'd been in the Grainger house and he intended to use it as an opportunity to put an idea to Seth. He was sure that it would result in the job being offered to him permanently. He hadn't been able to believe his luck when he was given the job, because old Seth had two sons to take over the reins. Now one son was wanted for a killing and the other one had neither the ability nor inclination to run a ranch or issue orders to rough ranch hands.

As Friedel stood before him after declining an invitation to sit, Seth was reminded how much he looked like his eldest son, Scott, with the same-coloured hair, rugged features and a similar, thickset build. Seth insisted that

Friedel should take a seat, jokingly saying that he didn't like his employees looking down on him.

Freidel looked concerned as he sat down, sensing that something was wrong. 'Is everything all right, Mr Grainger?' he asked. 'We were a bit late with the branding because one of the herd fell and broke a leg while we were rounding them up.'

'No, there's not a problem, Jeff. It's more of a personal matter. Well, personal to me, that is. I've just heard that my son is probably dead.'

'That's a real shame, Mr Grainger!' said Friedel, showing exaggerated concern before he added, 'I expect you always knew that the law would catch up with Scott one day.'

'It's Leo, not Scott.'

'How did it happen?' Friedel asked, showing his surprise, 'I thought he'd gone off to do a bit of travelling. Was it an accident?'

'No, it wasn't an accident, but I don't want to discuss it. The real reason that I have asked you to come here is to tell you how much I appreciate the hard work that you've put in.'

'It's a privilege working for you, Mr Grainger, and I've learned so much from you.'

'The thing is, Jeff, my son Scott will be coming home and taking over the foreman's job again.'

For a moment Friedel was lost for words as it sunk in that his plans lay in ruins. He wanted to tell old man Grainger that it wasn't fair, but he composed himself before he said, 'But I don't understand, Mr Grainger. How can he? He's a wanted man and they'll hang him if he shows his face here.'

'There's been a terrible mistake, Jeff, and it will all be sorted out. I'm sure that Scott would like to keep you on as an assistant, but there'll have be a drop in your pay.'

'What sort of mistake?' Friedel asked, his voice showing the first signs of his disappointment.

'You don't need to concern yourself

with that, Friedel. I just thought that you should know in case you wanted to look elsewhere for a foreman's job. I don't expect it will be easy stepping down, but I would imagine it will take a few weeks before matters are sorted out and Scott is back in the swing of things.'

Friedel managed to keep his feelings in check when he told Grainger that he appreciated the offer to work under his son, but he would like to think things over and he might move on.

'I understand how disappointed you must be. Anyway, I expect you'll need to get back to the herd.'

Friedel got to his feet and fiddled with his Stetson before he thanked Grainger and headed for the door, but he was in for more disappointment when Grainger called out, 'Oh, and, Friedel, you had better choose another horse over the next few days, because Scott will be wanting the blue roan back. He lost his palomino when he was on his travels. I expect he'll be pleased to be reunited with his other horse.'

Friedel quietly closed the door behind him and hurried outside. The blue roan was tied to the hitch rail and its current master had just decided that he wasn't planning to give it back. He had killed before and he would kill again to keep his job as foreman. He just needed to find Scott Grainger.

★   ★   ★

Toad Stokes mopped up the remains of his fried eggs and beans with a piece of bread which drew a smile from Chuck Mellor, who owned Chuck's Diner.

Toad Stokes had spent a restless night thinking about his pa's insistence on their taking the law into their own hands. He had no intention of confronting Scott Grainger and while his pa was still sleeping off the effects of yesterday's drinking Toad had crept from the cabin and headed for the barn, after he had gathered a few belongings and raided the box in which his pa kept some spare money. It had seemed like a good idea to leave his pa to take care of Grainger. What did it matter if his pa got caught and hung? The way his pa had been coughing in the mornings lately he didn't have long for this world. Toad had been thinking lately that once his pa was gone he could sell up and have himself a bit of fun. Perhaps he'd travel around and meet a woman whom he might even marry. If he did he would make sure she could cook and bake like his old ma used to. He'd sampled the saloon girls in town, but they were not the kind you'd want to marry and some of them had giggled at him when they'd pulled down his long johns. The only problem with leaving now was that if his pa did live longer than expected and carried on with his drinking he would likely lose his property to the bank and there would be nothing to return to.

Chuck was munching into one of his own sausages sandwiched between two crusty pieces of bread while looking out of the window when Toad rose from his chair and thanked him for the meal. He had just decided that he would kill Scott Grainger.

'Are you planning on leaving town, Toad? Your horse looks all loaded up. You wouldn't be aiming on doing a bit of buffalo hunting or gold prospecting, would you?' Chuck let out a hearty laugh and his rotund frame shook while bits of bread and sausage sprayed the window. He had never met anyone as bone idle as Toad Stokes; he would be more likely to eat a buffalo than hunt for them, and he wouldn't last a day panhandling.

Toad could tell a pack of lies with ease and he did when he told Chuck that he was riding over to his Uncle Herbert's place to deliver some clothes that he'd left behind after his last visit.

'Remember me to Herbert. Now there's a man with an appetite. If he lived in this town I'd be a rich man.' Chuck roared with laughter again and his flabby face turned red and his eyes watered.

Toad smiled. He didn't know why because he didn't find anything funny, but it didn't take much for Chuck to start guffawing.

Chuck wiped the grease from his chin with the back of his hand as he watched Toad ride off in the opposite direction to where Toad's Uncle Herbert lived. 'That feller's as dopey as they come,' he muttered to himself.

Toad had figured that it would be worth staking out the approach trail to the Grainger place, hoping that Scott would pass by and he'd be waiting. His pa wouldn't be fussed how Scott Grainger died and he would settle for a shot in the back just like Grainger had done to his brother. Toad heeled his horse into a gallop because now he could see an opportunity to impress his pa and still live an easy life at home. With Grainger dead his pa would give up the drinking and get back to running the place. Toad's future would be secured. He might even go calling on Emma Linton when everything had settled down, because maybe those stories about her were true and he wouldn't need to spend his pa's money on saloon girls.

18

Mackenzie gripped the bars of his cell. If it had been humanly possible he would have pulled them apart, driven by anger after he'd just overheard a conversation by the two deputies. No wonder the marshal had not been concerned about the threat of his buddy breaking him out of jail. Scott Grainger wouldn't be coming to his rescue.

Someone had slipped a note under the marshal's office door warning about the planned robbery. That was why the marshal and his deputy had been waiting at the bank. It also explained why Grainger was nowhere to be seen when Mackenzie had been pushed out of the bank on to the sidewalk with a pistol prodded into his back. Grainger was the only other person who knew about the planned robbery, so it had to have been he who had delivered the note when no one was about in case he was seen and arrested. Mackenzie didn't know why Grainger had double-crossed him, but it didn't matter because Grainger would soon be dead.

Mackenzie's anger was still raging when the deputy called to check on him and ask if he wanted a drink. Mackenzie was in luck because the deputy was no more than a kid and a greenhorn to boot. He went by the name of Lance Monkton, but Dopey would have been more fitting. Lance Monkton was the mayor's nephew and the mayor, who was his guardian, hoped the job would help toughen him up. Bordon Valley was a fairly quiet town and he knew that Marshal Stephens would look after him.

'Hey, kid, you are going to make a great marshal one day. You're a natural and I should know. I've lost count of the number of jails I've been in and I've met some fine lawmen, but you're the real deal.'

'Do you really think so?' the deputy asked. He'd never been complimented before and always seemed to be getting hollered at by the marshal, so it was nice to hear some encouraging words for a change.

'Sure do.'

'So can I get you a coffee?' the deputy asked, eager to repay the kind words.

'No thanks, but you could help fill in a few gaps about the folks in this town. My buddy, Scott Grainger, mentioned a sweet girl by the name of Emma. Does she live in town?'

'Emma Linton, you mean? No, she doesn't live in town. She lives with her pa about three miles out of town just off the trail to Coppinger's Creek. Your buddy's pa lives close by and just off the same trail.'

Mackenzie was wondering what the double-crossing Grainger was up to because he'd said he didn't have a pa. He smiled at the deputy and said, 'Thanks, Marshal. I was just curious.'

Lance sort of giggled and said, 'I'm

not the marshal.'

'But you soon will be when that old-timer hangs up his guns.'

'I'd better be getting on with my chores. Just give me a holler if you want a drink.'

Lance turned and was about to leave the cell area when Mackenzie called out, 'Hey, Marshal, I'd be obliged if you could empty my piss-pot while you're here. The smell from it is beginning to make my eyes water. I'm surprised you don't get a whiff of it out in your office. It must be all those beans you keep feeding me.'

Lance looked awkward when he explained that he wasn't allowed to open the cell unless another deputy was standing by.

'I wouldn't want to get you into trouble. So when's your buddy coming back?'

'Not until much later,' replied the deputy, He looked worried because the marshal had left strict instructions that both deputies should stay in the office except for a very short break. Now he was regretting agreeing to let the other deputy go off and meet up with the girl he was courting. The marshal was having a day at home catching up with some paperwork, so at least there shouldn't be any danger of him calling in.

'Hmmm. We've got a problem then, Deputy, because I think I need to go real soon and I don't mean for a pee.' Mackenzie screwed up his face and added. 'It must be all that talk about beans.'

'Promise me you won't try anything if I open the cell.'

'On my old ma's life and may the good Lord strike me down. I'll just sit over there on the bed and put my hands on my head if you like. But you'd better hurry, Deputy, or I'll be needing some fresh pants.'

The deputy's face showed his panic as he fumbled with the keys. The door was barely opened when he crashed to the floor after being kneed between his legs. Then his own gun was lifted from its holsters and smashed into the side of his face.

'Dumb-ass.' Mackenzie sniggered as he knelt down and unbuckled the deputy's gunbelt and fastened it around his own waist. He quickly left the cell, closed the door behind him and removed the keys. Once in the main office he peered through the window to see if the coast was clear and couldn't believe his luck when he saw a horse tied to the hitch rail outside.

Main Street was quiet apart from a few folks chinwagging outside the store. None paid him any attention as he eased his stolen horse into a gentle trot down the street in the direction of the trail that led to Coppinger's Creek. He would soon be spurring the horse into a gallop on his way to settle a score with that double-dealing bastard, Scott Grainger. If he couldn't find him, then he would go looking for his lady love, Miss Emma Linton. At least he'd have a bit of pleasure as his way of getting even with Grainger.

19

Toad Stokes had figured that Scott would likely appear at his pa's place at some point, but wouldn't be dumb enough to stay there. He'd ridden close by and saw old Seth working out front, but there was no sign of Scott, so he rode back a short distance along the trail, tethered his horse's reins to the overhanging branch of a small plains cottonwood tree and hid behind some rocks.

* * *

Toad dropped his rifle when he awoke from his snooze after drinking half a bottle of whiskey and munching his way through most of the food supplies in his saddle-bags. He'd bought the supplies in town before he went to the diner, intending to take them on his journey, before he'd changed his mind about leaving. He was on the point of nodding off again when he spotted a rider coming his way. He shook his head, rubbed his eyes to wake himself up and took a swig of whiskey before he picked up his rifle and trained it on the approaching rider. He was on a different horse, but it was definitely Scott Grainger, God's gift to women. Perhaps it was the effect of the whiskey that made Toad calm as he prepared to shoot someone for the first time. 'This is for my brother,' Toad muttered to himself. He fired off a shot that found its target and the rider thudded to the ground. Toad punched the air and let out a cry of delight. It had been so easy and there were no witnesses. He would say that he tried to arrest Grainger, who had resisted and then gone for his gun. That was when Toad had shot him. Toad mounted his horse and heeled it in the direction of town. Within half an hour he would swagger into the saloon and tell everyone how he had avenged his brother's killing. The saloon girls would give him admiring looks and he would fill himself with beer and whiskey before he headed home to tell his pa that he had come face to face with Scott Grainger and killed him.

★ ★ ★

Leo Grainger had waited patiently on the hill that looked down on the Lintons' log cabin, which was much smaller than his pa's ranch house but in the same valley. John Linton owned a printing press in Bordon, but he preferred to live away from the town, him being a private man. Grainger's heart quickened when he saw John Linton being waved off by Emma. She was too far away for him to see her clearly, but he could still picture her beauty, just as he had almost every day since she'd blossomed into a shapely woman. So much had happened since the last time he'd spoken to her and he'd been too shy to declare his feelings, but soon he would find out whether good fortune would bless him once again. Emma had a heart of gold and she of all people would not be repulsed or deterred by his disfigurement. She had not fallen for the charms of his brother, who could have had his pick of any of the women in town. She must believe that what was in a man's heart and character was more important than how handsome he was.

He had remained on horseback while he'd kept watch; now he eased his mount behind the trees as John Linton passed close by, then he saw him gallop off into the distance. He would be patient and wait to make sure that Linton didn't turn back, having forgotten something, but he was surprised when he saw that Emma had come from behind the house on her red roan and was riding off. For a moment he was uncertain what to do, then he heeled his horse to give chase. Emma was a fine horsewoman and Josie's horse, which he was riding, was tired from the long journey home and was no match for Emma's fine animal. His only hope of catching up with her was if she stopped to sit and survey the scenery, which he knew she was fond of doing; but he was in for a disappointment when she slowed down her mount, turned off the main trails and entered the narrow track. It was the track that led to his pa's ranch. He urged his mount on, but when he approached the house where he had been born Emma had already dismounted and was climbing the steps to the porch.

He watched her tap on the door with her riding whip, then, deciding there was no one at home, turn and make her way down the steps. She was about to put her foot in her horse's stirrup when she saw him. She appeared puzzled, as though she was looking at a stranger.

He had rehearsed so many times what he would say, but now he struggled because of her expression.

'Emma, it's me, Leo.'

'Leo, I didn't . . . ' she didn't finish,

realizing that he might be offended.

'Recognize me.' He completed it for her.

'No, I'm sorry, but Scott told me that you were probably dead. So I was just shocked.' Emma partly lied to spare his feelings as she looked closer at his face.

Leo wasn't prepared for the possibility that his brother had been in touch with Emma and he struggled to control his emotions.

'What did he want?' asked Leo, his question sounding more of a demand than an enquiry.

'It's meant to be a secret, but I don't suppose he'd mind me telling you.'

Emma paused and he could tell by her smile that it was going to be something that he didn't want to hear.

'He's asked me to marry him,' she blurted out excitedly, more in the manner of a young girl than the full-bodied woman that she'd become.

'Surely your pa won't let you marry a killer?'

'My daddy doesn't know about

Scott's proposal yet. Scott swore to me that he didn't kill Donny Stokes, but he knows who did. I came here to give him my answer. He told me that if I agree to marry him he'll go to Marshal Stephens and it will all be cleared up.'

Leo struggled to calm himself as the news settled in. It meant that his plans were in tatters, ruined by the brother whom he'd grown to hate.

'Emma, let's go inside and wait for Scott, but before he comes home there are things you need to be told about my brother.'

Emma's face saddened. Her happy mood seemed threatened, but she needed to hear what Leo meant, so she turned and headed up the steps, followed by Leo. She had never been inside the Grainger home and although it looked clean she could see that it was missing a woman's touch. It was much, much bigger than her pa's place, with a large hallway and a lot more rooms. She guessed that this was where she would live if she married Scott. Leo directed her to the living room and invited her to sit in one of the leather upholstered chairs. He waited until she was settled in it before he spoke.

'Scott is lying when he told you he didn't kill Donny. He confessed to me just before he rode off. He wanted me to lie for him and tell the marshal that he'd left days earlier, but I couldn't do it. He killed a man, Emma, just because he was jealous that you might have feelings for him. He'll make your life hell with his jealousy and he won't be able to stop lusting after saloon girls. He even threatened me once because I told him how much I liked you, but I more than like you, Emma, and there's something that you need to know about my feelings for you. I love — '

Emma looked troubled as she interrupted him and said, 'Leo, I'm going to marry Scott. I came to tell him that the answer is yes. I'm sorry, but it's Scott that I love and I think I always have.'

Leo's face filled with a look of desperation, 'I've just told you, Emma, that you don't know the real Scott, nor does my pa and that's why I went to bring Scott back and make him tell the truth. You've got to listen to me for your own good.'

★   ★   ★

Scott Grainger had hoped to avoid meeting John Linton until he'd spoken to Emma again, but the two men were within eye contact when Scott rounded the bend that led to his pa's ranch house.

'Howdy, Mr Linton,' Scott called out politely.

'You've got some nerve coming back here, Grainger, but if you harm my daughter with any sweet-talking then I swear to God that I'll kill you.'

'You've got me figured all wrong, because your sweet daughter is just about the last person on earth that I would hurt,' Grainger replied, disappointed at the hostility and venom shown by Linton.

197

'Fancy words, but if you meant them then you would let her be. What future could she have with a man who faces a rope or a bullet from someone who wants revenge! By the way, the Stokes family know you are back, I made sure of that, and they'll be gunning for you. So maybe you'll run away just like you did after shooting Donny Stokes in the back.'

'I ain't running anywhere and I might be seeing you later, but I need to see Emma first.'

Scott heeled his horse into motion and didn't look back. If he had he would have seen that John Linton was following him.

Grainger had been taken aback by the anger shown by John Linton, who had just joined the list of those who wanted him dead. He had already come face to face with a man who he hadn't figured would be on the list less than ten minutes earlier.

Grainger steered his horse to start the slow ride down the hill and saw

Emma run from his pa's house, stumble down the steps of the porch, then run on. She was being chased by a man and she was trying to undo the small bag she always carried with her. Grainger urged his mount forward. He sensed movement in the bushes to his right, but concentrated on riding down to Emma at a speed that was not sensible on such a slope. He paid the price when he was thrown from his horse as it stumbled. He fell heavily on to his shoulder and for a moment he was badly winded and struggled to get to his feet. He shook his head, still dazed by the effects of his fall and realized that it was his brother, Leo, who was trying to pull Emma back towards the house. Scott shouted as he ran, but his brother seemed oblivious to him approaching. Then, when he saw him, he drew his pistol and fired. The bullet thudded into Scott's chest and he fell to the ground. Leo's face was filled with hate as he looked down and pointed the pistol at his hapless brother's head. The volley of gunfire left both the Grainger brothers lying within a few feet of each other. One was already dead; the other was close to it as the blood ran through fingers that clutched his wound; his face was already pale from the shock. Emma had slumped to the ground, sobbing and shivering, unaware of the commotion above her. She was still clutching the small pistol she had eventually pulled from her handbag, unaware that just a short distance away the marshal had just arrested two men, both of whom had intended to kill Scott Grainger. Emma's dreams had been shattered in such a short time that had seen joy turn to grief: she would never marry Scott Grainger.

20

Marshal Stephens sipped the hot coffee that Deputy Ike Naylor had just brewed. He couldn't remember ever having a father and son in the same cell and next to one with such an upright man as John Linton in it.

'So what's going to happen to them, Marshal?'

The marshal gave a heavy sigh before replying. 'It'll be up to a jury, but two of them will end their days at the end of a rope. Toad Stokes's case is straightforward enough. You arrested him in the saloon when he was bragging about shooting Scott Grainger. Some would say good riddance to Mackenzie, but it's no excuse just because he killed the wrong man. Toad was never the brightest of people and he always did have a big mouth when he had a few drinks inside him.'

The deputy smiled, 'I remember when me and Toad got our first guns and we did some target shooting up near Crawley Rocks. It was just firing at cans and Toad didn't hit a single can even when he moved real close to them. Me and Hank Weaver couldn't stop hootin' and Hank nearly peed in his pants. Toad told us that he'd always had trouble with his eyes, just like his pa, so Toad must have been real close to Mackenzie when he shot him.'

Deputy Naylor was still feeling a mite sorry for the other deputy who had been hoodwinked and hurt by Mackenzie. Naylor had received a verbal bashing from the marshal for leaving young Lance Monkton on his own and had been told he'd be looking for another job the next time he disobeyed instructions. The marshal had been patient with Monkton; he'd already told the mayor that his nephew wasn't cut out for the job, but he'd said he could keep his badge as a souvenir.

'So who killed the Grainger brother

who is already dead?'

'We will never know because Linton and Stokes both admit that they intended to kill Scott Grainger and fired down the hill at him. According to Doc Bennett Seth will be burying two sons tomorrow.'

Ike looked puzzled again when he asked, 'So did Scott kill Donny Stokes like his brother said?'

'Hmmm, now that's another puzzle that we probably won't ever be able to solve. I guess he did because why would he leave town just after, but then again, why would he come back and why would he risk being arrested when he'd tipped me off about the robbery? Lance told me that Mackenzie had revealed that Scott was his buddy, so it had to be him who placed the note under the door.'

'There are lots of unanswered questions, Marshal, and I think it's unfair the way folks blame Miss Linton for causing all the trouble. She isn't a flirt like they say.'

'I never had you down as an authority on womenfolk, Naylor,' said the marshal with a smile.

'I'm not,' replied the deputy and tried to hide his embarrassment when he added, 'I just think she's a sweet girl and probably doesn't even realize what a beauty she is.' Naylor decided to change the subject and asked the marshal if he would be attending the funerals.

'I'll be there to give Seth some support. We go back a long way and he has no other kinfolk. I don't suppose he ever thought he would outlive his children.'

'If it's a double funeral will they bury the Grainger brothers in the same grave?' Naylor enquired.

'You do ask some odd questions, Naylor. I wouldn't have thought Reverend Langford would encourage that. He would probably see it as good and evil being in the same grave and that wouldn't sit comfortably with him, but we'll have to wait and see.'

* ★ ★

Seth Grainger appeared to have aged in just a few days as he stood by the graveside for the second funeral of the day. His face was drawn and his shoulders hunched as the Reverend David Langford, who was not much older than his own sons, said his piece. Seth couldn't help feeling responsible. Perhaps if he'd handled things differently two young men would still be alive. He'd gone over in his mind the last time he'd spoken to them and tried to make excuses, but it didn't help. He'd given a cursory nod to Emma Linton, whom he was surprised to see at the small gathering. She was wearing a long black dress with silk attachments and not even her fiercest critics could accuse her of flaunting herself today. The black net was covering her ashen face and eyes that were still red from crying. She was still shaking from the shock of seeing the Grainger brothers lying in separate pools of blood.

Seth Grainger didn't take in a single word of the fine tribute the minister paid to his son, because his eyes were fixed on the grave next to the gaping hole where the coffin would soon be lowered. The other grave was the resting place of his beloved wife, Audrey. The tears slowly trickled down his face as he silently begged her forgiveness for not doing more to stop things ending in the tragic way that they had.

Marshal Stephens had given Seth a few words of comfort before the mourners dispersed and left him alone by the graveside. Had they stayed they would have seen him sobbing, but they wouldn't have known that his troubles were far from over.

21

Seth Grainger was still wearing the same black suit that he'd worn at the cemetery a few days earlier when he entered Marshal Stephens's office. Now the suit was creased and crumpled and it seemed likely that Seth had slept in it, if his troubled mind had allowed him to sleep. He'd always dreaded the prospect of losing a son because of the violent world that he'd witnessed, but could never have imagined that it would happen the way it had.

Seth had always been a reserved man and he looked uncomfortable as he stood in front of Marshal Stephen's desk before Stephens invited him to take a seat. After the marshal had asked him how he was coping he enquired, 'So what brings you here, Seth? I hope you're not looking to cause trouble with your son's killer, whoever that may be.'

'I'm not here to cause trouble, Marshal, but I would like to speak to you alone,' Seth said, looking at the deputy who was thumbing through some paperwork. The marshal waited for his deputy to take the hint and when he didn't he told him to go and fill his face in the diner.

Deputy Naylor placed a bundle of papers on the desk and headed for the door like a boy who has just been let out of school early and invited to dip his hand in a jar of cookies.

Seth waited until the door was closed behind the departing deputy before he cleared his throat and spoke.

'Marshal, I have something very important to tell you, and I want to ask you a big favour.'

'If I can help you in any way, Seth, then you know I will.'

'Neither Tobias Stokes nor John Linton killed my son. I know who did, but it needs some explaining.'

Marshal Stephens wasn't an easy man to shock, but he was shocked now as he invited Seth to take his time.

When Seth had finished his explanation the marshal eyed Seth sympathetically and feared that all the upset had affected him. The two men in custody had admitted shooting and it didn't matter what they intended to do, but Seth Grainger hadn't finished and had more revelations, which left the marshal with a feeling of disbelief.

'Jesus, Seth, is there anything else that you want to tell me?' the marshal asked, then scratched his head, wondering how he could handle all this.

'Are you absolutely sure about this, Seth?' enquired the marshal, needing to confirm at least some of what he'd just been told.

'They didn't even find their target and I think if Doc Bennett shows you the bullet he dug out of my son it won't have been fired from either of the rifles used by Stokes or Linton, or any other rifle for that matter.'

'Well, I'll be damned. You would have made a good Pilkington detective, Seth. I was a bit puzzled why they hadn't tried to shoot Scott when he rode by at the top of the hill. Apparently Tobias Stokes had been waiting for some time and had fallen asleep. He only woke up when Scott was already heading down the hill and Linton told me that he had only just arrived at the spot.' The marshal paused briefly, then he agreed to the favour Seth had asked and revealed some of his own thoughts.

'Emma Linton must be going through hell after all that's happened, but Stokes and her pa will still face a trial because they have already admitted that they fired at Scott. Tobias Stokes has been all screwed up since his son was killed and I can understand why he might want to take his revenge on the man he thought had done it, but it was still wrong. Linton is a different matter and some folks have always been concerned about him being so overprotective towards his girl. Some men will never consider a man good enough for their daughter, but they don't try to kill the ones they disapprove of.'

'I must admit that I've never liked

Linton,' said Seth Grainger of the man whom he might just have saved from a hanging. 'I know he used to give his wife a hard time and seemed ashamed just because she had been a saloon girl, even though she was only a singer.'

'He's never been my favourite person,' the marshal replied in agreement. 'Talking of saloon girls, I had a feller come in this morning and tell me some sad news. Do you remember Josie Tolman, who used to work in the saloon when it first opened?'

Seth looked thoughtful for a moment and then he remembered the girl from the time he used to join his men after they came home from a cattle drive. He told the marshal that he recalled her.

'He told me that he'd called in at the Tolman homestead near Gatow Crossing which is now a ghost town since the railroad workers moved on. He found Josie lying on her own bed. She'd been smothered with a pillow. Josie must have worked in just about every saloon this side of the Crookham River and a few more besides, I shouldn't wonder. I think I met her husband once and I recall he was a miserable son of a bitch, a bit like Linton, but it seems he left Josie a while back.'

'Do you think her husband killed her?'

'Who knows, but the feller who told me about Josie also told me that the bodies of two of Josie's neighbours had been found lying near the Crookham River crossing. They'd both been shot in the back.'

'Josie always was a fun-loving girl and I'm sad to hear what happened to her,' sympathized Grainger, despite his own grief.

The marshal gave a heavy sigh and said, 'It's been all doom and gloom news here this morning. Look at this.'

The marshal pushed the *Elmore County Gazette* newspaper towards Grainger and pointed to the front page headline that read: Train Disaster — Death Toll 87. The marshal was grim-faced when he said, 'The train heading for Drover City came off a bridge that crosses over the

Crookham River. Only one man survived, most of those killed were trapped inside the carriages. There was a woman and her two young daughters among the poor victims.'

The marshal continued talking while Seth was skimming through the article.

'That woman's husband is the president of the railway company. He goes by the name of Stanmore Poulson and there's talk of him running for governor. The ironic thing is that the bridge is named after him.'

Grainger didn't bother to read the full article and asked the marshal whether they knew the cause of the accident.

'The bridge just collapsed. It might have been tampered with by robbers who planned to halt the train as it approached the bridge. There are also rumours that it was sabotaged by former workers who helped build the bridge and were promised big bonuses and a resettlement package by the company. It seems that Poulson is a ruthless businessman and he reneged on the deal. I remember hearing about a big demonstration down near Fort Hewson where the army had to be called in because of some angry settlers who had built homesteads under the land claim scheme. Some had sweated blood and tears working the land and they got evicted when the rail company took the land back through some dirty legal dealings. I wonder whether the Poulson feller was involved in that. Anyway, I expect you'll want to be doing a few chores while you're in town, Seth. And don't worry about that favour, but you know I can't wait too long.'

'I'm much obliged, Marshal, and I'm glad I told you because it's been bothering me some. I just needed to attend to the funerals, but I've already explained that. Good day to you, Marshal.'

The marshal watched the forlorn figure trudge from his office. He was thinking that no man deserved to lose both his sons the way Seth was about to.

22

Tobias Oakes had been allowed to attend the funeral of his son Toad, who had been found guilty of Mackenzie's murder and hanged. Only officials and Reverend Langford had attended Toad's hanging, but Chuck Mellor had closed his diner to join Tobias at Toad's funeral and mourn the loss of his favourite customer.

Toad was buried next to his brother, Donny. Tobias Oakes wept like a baby and only the deputies prevented him from crashing down on to his son's coffin as it was lowered in to the grave. Tobias blamed himself for Toad's death, knowing that if he hadn't have goaded his son into seeking revenge for his brother's death then he would still be alive today.

Tobias Oakes's guilt couldn't be eased by the effects of whiskey as he awaited his own trial. He hoped an end to his torture would come when he was hanged and laid to rest near his sons. He hadn't understood what the marshal had meant when he said that perhaps he wouldn't hang after all. The marshal couldn't go into detail except to say that he thought Tobias should know. The thought of a reprieve from the noose wasn't what Tobias wanted to hear.

John Linton occupied the cell next to Tobias Oakes, but they never spoke a word to each other. Oakes was still convinced that Emma Linton had been the cause of all the trouble. His wife Agnes had always dressed in a prim and proper fashion, not like Emma Linton, who exposed parts of her flesh that should only be seen by a husband or a doctor. Linton had begged the marshal to persuade his daughter to visit him so that he could explain that he'd only wanted to protect her. Each time he heard someone approach the cells his hopes were raised that his beautiful daughter would emerge, but she never did. The marshal didn't have the heart to tell him that his daughter might soon be facing troubles of her own.

★ ★ ★

Judge John James Tovey had presided over the trial of Toad Oakes, but it was nearly two months later when he returned to Bordon Valley to preside over three trials, starting with those of Tobias Oakes and John Linton. The judge would be retiring at the conclusion of the last of the three cases and many of the press had arrived from the big cities to report the trials, including one from the East. The judge had mellowed in the last few years and shown a compassionate side that had not been present throughout most of his career, during which he had sentenced ninety-seven men to death. Men were taking bets in the saloon that the old judge would make sure that the juries delivered the verdicts that would see the figure rounded up to a century.

For those who knew that Judge Tovey liked order and neatness in his life they believed that recording a century of hangings would appeal to him.

Tobias Oakes was tried first. His defence attorney had ignored his client's wishes and pleaded that Tobias had suffered enough through the loss of his two sons. He demonstrated in court that Oakes's eyesight was so poor that he would not have been capable of hitting a target ten times the size of a man from his vantage point near the scene of the killing on the Grainger property. The sympathetic jury took pity on him because of the death of both his sons and duly found him not guilty. If Judge Tovey was disappointed with the verdict then he hid it well when he ordered Oakes's release. Oakes left the courtroom feeling that the court had let him down and now he would have to decide how he himself would put an end to his misery.

★ ★ ★

At the start of the trial of John Linton, the judge explained to the court that evidence had been produced that would have special significance. The prosecution counsel scornfully dismissed Linton's claim that he hadn't really meant to kill Scott Grainger that day, but merely wound him to serve as a warning to stay away from his daughter, Emma. The prosecutor said that Linton must be the finest marksman in the whole of the state if he could guarantee to only wound a man from such a great distance. Under the direction of the judge the jury found Grainger guilty of a lesser charge because Doc Bennett had testified that the bullet fired by Linton had not found its target. Linton was still sentenced to seven years in the state prison at Ashworth, situated in the remotest part of Wyoming. As Linton had been led from the courtroom he had scanned the gathering, hoping to see his daughter, Emma, but he didn't. He would never see her again.

23

Judge Tovey looked embarrassed when he was clapped by just about everyone in the courtroom as he sat down after the announcement by the clerk of the court that it was to be the judge's last case. The judge had gone over the papers in his hotel room the previous evening and he couldn't remember having presided over such an unusual and difficult case as this was likely going to be.

Marshal Stephens was seated near the front row. He had kept his promise, but now he had some regrets that he hadn't used his discretion and prevented the possibility of another hanging. He had spent many hours deliberating what he should do and eventually reminded himself that it was for others to judge. The mayor had demanded to know who was on trial today and why hadn't that person been locked in one of the cells. The marshal had refused to reveal who it was, the town was rife with speculation and bets had been placed. There had been a late flurry of money on it being Emma Linton, because she was the only other person close enough to have killed one of the men who wanted to marry her. The marshal had revealed to some folks that when he arrived at the scene Emma was clutching a small pistol. It was the pistol that her pa had insisted that she always carried with her for protection against lustful men.

Merle L. Jarrod, the prosecuting counsel, was forty-two years old and always stood ramrod upright as though attempting to make the most of his medium stature. The moustache was trimmed daily and the long nose and jutting jaw gave an appearance of arrogance. Jarrod's philosophy was simple and that was to do his utmost to ensure that the defendant in every case was found guilty. Jarrod did not concern himself with morals and justice; it was simply a contest of skills between him and the defendant's counsel. He didn't really think that he would have much difficulty today as he shook hands with Samuel Sampson, the defence attorney.

Sampson was thirty-one years old, tall and gangly with schoolboy features and a wispy goatee beard the very survival of which would be threatened in a high wind. This was Sampson's first murder trial and Jarrod smirked when he saw his opponent's obvious nervousness.

Judge Tovey went though the preliminaries and then announced that because of special circumstances normal procedures would not be followed regarding when the accused and witnesses would take the stand. He said this had been discussed and agreed with both the prosecuting and defence attorneys.

When the clerk of the court duly called for the accused to take the stand all eyes were on the three people who were in the specially allocated area next to where the defence counsel was seated. One of them wore a pretty scarlet dress. Her hair had grown longer and nestled on her shoulders. The light-blue eyes were clear, the redness from crying was no longer there and she was as beautiful as ever. Many of the men in court kept their eyes fixed on her while some women muttered to each other, dismissing her as a harlot. The figure in the middle looked forlorn and his appearance shocked those who hadn't seen him for some months. His face was drawn, his hair uncombed and he seemed to be in a trance. It was Seth Grainger. The young man to his right was subdued and still not fully recovered from his injuries.

When the clerk of the court boomed out his order for the defendant to take the stand, the suspense could be felt throughout the court. Some were ready to say, 'I told you so!' while others were anticipating their winnings, willing Emma Linton to stand up. Emma Linton and Scott Grainger rose from their seats at the same time and there were lots of open mouths around the court at the shock of the unexpected sight.

Someone muttered that two people couldn't take the stand together. Others wondered what would happen to their stake money if two people were guilty of the killing. Emma and Scott stood either side of Seth Grainger and helped him to his feet.

'Take your time, Pa,' Scott whispered in Seth's ear. Seth nodded to indicate that he was all right and the two young people each took hold of one of Seth's arms and slowly escorted him to the stand and eased him into the specially provided chair. His shoulders drooped, no longer the man who would stare down even the roughest and meanest cowboy.

The clerk of the court was about to ask Seth to take the oath when the judge raised a hand to stop him, then cleared his throat before he made a special announcement to the court. He told the gathering that the defendant's identity had been kept a secret for fear that such an unusual case might generate such a massive interest that the town would be flooded with outsiders and might create a public order problem. He went on to explain that the accused had suffered a condition known as a stroke and it had left him with restricted mobility and that was why he was accompanied by helpers to assist him. The judge finished his explanation and indicated to the clerk of the court to continue.

Seth Grainger's voice wavered as he took the oath and when, a few minutes later, Seth Grainger pleaded not guilty to murdering his son Leo there were loud murmurings around the court.

Jarrod put on his most serious expression, which he had practised in front of the mirror in his hotel room before he left for the court, and began his opening address.

'I am certain that most of the fine people of this town, especially the respected members of the jury, will agree that the taking of a life can rarely be justified unless it was in order to save one's own life. Seth Grainger's life had not been in danger on the day he shot his younger son in cold blood. He shot and killed a good and caring son, who had been the victim of the most brutal attack that anyone could imagine while searching for his wanted brother. Leo Grainger had returned home hoping for the love and protection of his family and to marry a young woman that he worshipped. He was spurned by a heartless woman and fatally wounded by his own father, who wanted to save the life of a wild and reckless son.'

Jarrod had turned to look in the direction of where Scott Grainger was sitting. He paused long enough for it to register with the jury, then continued.

'This man became a member of the ruthless and murderous Mackenzie gang, but claims he never committed any crime while he was with them. It seems that the only person in the whole wide world who believes Scott Grainger is innocent of doing any wrong is his father, who stands before us today.'

When Seth Grainger was sworn in his voice had been weak, but now he met the stare that was being delivered by Jarrod.

'I wouldn't imagine that you sleep very well, Mr Grainger,' Jarrod said. It was more of a statement than a question and he quickly added, 'I would wager that there is not another man in this court who would shoot his own son from behind like you did. So, I guess that makes you rather special in a not very desirable way.'

Grainger showed some discomfort for the first time and he didn't hear Jarrod's question which followed.

'Do you believe in God, Mr Grainger?'

When Grainger didn't reply Jarrod made the most of it when he continued, 'I expect that you don't, but perhaps your thoughts were elsewhere, so I will ask you again. Do you believe in God?'

Grainger was quick to reply and he faced the jury when he did just as his attorney had advised him to. 'My faith in the Lord has been tested on occasions.

Not just by recent events, but when we lost a dear sweet daughter when she was three years old and again when my dearest wife, Audrey, was taken from me. But the answer is, yes, I do believe in the Lord.'

'And yet you took a life by making a decision that Godfearing folk would say wasn't yours to take?'

Jarrod's questioning continued at length, but he carefully avoided asking Seth to explain why he fired the fatal shot that took his own son's life. Jarrod had had one of his assistants check out the jury and discovered that with one exception the jury comprised serious churchgoing folk. He was satisfied that he had exposed Seth Grainger as someone who had killed in a most ruthless way and played God. Jarrod kept his serious expression when he declared that he had finished questioning the defendant and returned to his seat, but he still had a surprise up his sleeve.

The judge announced that in view of Seth Grainger's medical condition he would be recalled to the stand later for cross examination by the defence counsel. Seth Grainger looked even frailer as he was helped back to his seat by his son and Emma Linton.

When Seth was seated Jarrod was invited to call his witness. When he did so the town's minister, Reverend David Langford, made his way to the stand. The gasps of shock around the court were followed by cries of, 'No!' and 'Shame!' when the minister was asked to take the oath. Many grew angry as they shouted their disapproval that a man of God should be asked to take the oath.

Judge Tovey rarely used his gavel, but he did now, perhaps thinking it would be his last opportunity. The court returned to silence, but some of the gathering responded more to the calming hand-gesture of the minister than the gavel, and the court room was quiet again. The minister nodded towards a section that was made up of members of his congregation as if to acknowledge their response to him, then he looked serious as he began taking the oath.

Jarrod thanked the minister for attending and being so dignified and an example to everyone. He then asked the minister what was to be his only question.

'Reverend Langford, can you imagine any circumstances where the Lord would approve the taking of a life?'

The minister was a small-framed man, with a large, almost round face and protruding teeth that had been the butt of many jokes when he was a boy and still continued behind his back. He was also rather shy, but his shyness disappeared when he was preaching and he frequently held the congregation spellbound with his sermons. He hesitated briefly before he answered the question while looking directly at Seth Grainger. 'No, sir, I cannot. Not even the Lord himself would do such a thing. All life is sacred in the eyes of the Lord, including the lives of the ungodly and disbelieving amongst us.'

Jarrod managed to hide his smugness, knowing that the respected minister's comments would have registered with the jury and Seth Grainger would end his days with a noose around his neck.

The judge called a short adjournment. When the court reconvened Seth Grainger was already on the stand, ready to be cross-examined by his defence counsel. Samuel Sampson's opening presentation for the defence case was woeful, mainly on account of his nervousness, and there were more mutterings around the court-room, but as he questioned Seth he grew in confidence. Seth revealed how one son was always fun-loving and, as he grew up, had become a bit wild. The other son was sly, moody, and had a jealous streak.

Samson asked Seth to describe what happened on the day he shot and killed his own son. Seth told how he had been working out back in the barn when he heard a woman screaming. He had hurried round to the front of the house and saw his son Scott running towards

Emma Linton. Emma was being chased by his other son, Leo, who drew his pistol and shot his brother. There were other shots, but he couldn't tell where they came from. Leo had moved towards his brother, who was lying on his back, blood oozing from his chest. Leo then pointed the gun at his brother with what appeared to be the intention of 'finishing him off'. Before he could fire his gun Seth had drawn his pistol and fired at Leo, hoping to just stop him, but the bullet hit him in the back of the head, killing him instantly.

There were tears in Seth's eyes as Sampson interrupted him and asked why he was wearing his pistol when working around the ranchhouse. Seth explained that there had been a spate of robberies and he was just being prepared in case the thieves came calling on him.

Seth was wiping the tears from his eyes when Sampson asked him to answer those who said that he had 'played God' in choosing to risk killing one son in the hope of saving another one.

'I just did what I thought was right. My son, Leo, was bad. On the day that he killed Donny Stokes — yes, it was Leo who killed Donny — he told a pack of lies. I had seen Leo ride off on his brother's horse that day. Scott came and told me that he was leaving for a while and he would explain when he came back and that Leo would tell him what it was all about. When I discovered that Leo had told the marshal that his brother had killed Stokes I knew he had lied, just like he had many times when he was growing up. Then when Scott came back he told me what had really happened. On the day that Donny Stokes was killed Leo had borrowed Scott's palomino and had come home in a frightened state. He told Scott that he had killed Donny Stokes and that someone had seen him riding away on Scott's horse. Scott suggested that he would leave town and if the marshal came looking for him in connection with the killing he was to tell him that Scott had left a few days earlier on the palomino and it must have been someone else riding another palomino who had killed Donny.'

'So Scott tried to save his brother from a hanging?' Sampson suggested.

'Yes, and it was wrong, but Leo said that he shot Stokes in self-defence. I found out later that Leo had shot him in the back. When the marshal came calling because Tim Buckley had seen Scott's palomino being ridden off close to where Stokes was gunned down, Leo lied and told the marshal that Scott had confessed to the killing.'

'So what did you think when Leo left home?'

'The day before he left I asked if he knew anything about Donny Stokes's killing that he wanted to tell me. He said he hadn't, but asked me why I always believed that Scott could do no wrong. I never actually accused him of lying, but I think he knew I had my suspicions. I thought he couldn't live with the shame of what he'd done and decided to start a new life somewhere else. The next time I saw him was the day he was about to kill his brother.'

Sampson announced that he had no further questions and sat down feeling satisfied that things had gone well. He took several sips from the glass of water on the small table and prepared to call his witness once Seth Grainger had been helped back to his seat.

In contrast to Sampson's, Jarrod's mood had changed and he began to fidget in his seat. Things hadn't gone as he'd expected and this young upstart defence counsel was good, he had to admit that. He would have to make sure that during the summing up he made it clear that the court only had Seth Grainger's word and that he had made up the story to stop his son Scott from facing a hanging for killing Donny Stokes. He would remind the court that Scott had confessed to killing Jeff Friedel over an argument about a horse. Jarrod's hopes of discrediting

Seth's testimony about his evil son were about to receive a setback when Sampson called his witness, Marshal Ed Stockman from Brunswick. Sampson had gone to see the marshal when Scott had told him that was where Leo had been during the last days of his search for him.

After Marshal Stockman had been sworn in Sampson asked him why he had felt sorry for Leo Grainger, even though he had been involved in a robbery in which two men had died. The marshal explained that he believed that Leo had been an unfortunate victim that had left him disfigured and facing a hanging because he was trying to reunite his killer brother with their dying father.

'We know that he lied about his father's condition, so why do you think he was trying to find his brother?'

The marshal sighed heavily and looked grave when he replied, 'I made a big mistake in showing him pity. I think he intended to find his brother and kill him, but I have another reason for regretting what I did and it probably cost a woman and two men their lives at the hands of Leo Grainger.'

There was a lot of shuffling and muttering. Jarrod's face had lost its confidence and Judge Tovey wondered what was coming next. Marshal Stockman explained that when he'd arrived in town a couple of days ago to attend the trial he had paid a courtesy call on the town's marshal. Marshal Stephens had shown him a water bottle with Stockman's name scratched on it. The bottle had been brought in by a man who had found it in the remote homestead of a woman named Josie Tolman. Josie Tolman's body had been discovered lying in her bed and she had been suffocated with a pillow. Marshal Stockman recognized it as the same water bottle that he had given Leo Grainger to take with on his train journey home.

Judge Tovey decided that he'd been patient enough with the young defence counsel and warned him that his witness's testimony did not prove that Leo Granger was connected with the murder of the woman. The presence of the bottle was not proof that Grainger had been there and he suggested that Grainger might have thrown the empty bottle from the train and it could have been picked up by someone.

'Do you have any other evidence that Leo Grainger was at Josie Tolman's homestead, even though you don't know why he would have left the train?' Sampson asked.

'I do, sir!' the marshal replied and then continued, 'After discussing the water bottle, Marshal Stephens and I inspected the horse that Leo Grainger was riding on the day he died. The horse bore the Tolman brand and it seems more than likely that he stole it after killing Josie Tolman.'

Jarrod jumped to his feet and protested at the marshal's speculation. Leo Grainger was not on trial here, he said, but his father was.

Sampson said that any evidence that

supported Seth Grainger's description of his dead son's character should be considered by the jury. Leo Grainger had undoubtedly suffered appalling injuries, but he had lied about his father dying and he had likely lied about many other matters that were more serious.

Marshal Stockman was the last witness and Jarrod's summing up for the prosecution lacked any real conviction and was rambling, unlike Sampson's, which was focused on the fact that Leo Grainger was just as his father had described, sly, perhaps even evil and a killer.

The jury took less than ten minutes to return a verdict of guilty and the court waited in lively expectancy for the judge's sentence. Jarrod had regained his arrogance and Sampson gave Grainger a sympathetic look.

Judge Tovey banged his gavel on the hard desk top and the mutterings that included, 'I told you he'd hang,' and 'Serves him right,' stopped. The judge cleared his throat before he spoke to the now hushed gathering.

'I never expected my last case to be the most unusual one that I have presided over in a long and I hope distinguished career. The defendant has been found guilty and there could have been no other verdict. The prosecution counsel attempted to portray the defendant as acting like the good Lord himself by taking a life, the life of his youngest son. The defence counsel attempted to expose the deceased as an evil man, suggesting that he might even have deserved to die. I am reminded that the defendant confessed to the killing when he need not have done and would have avoided appearing here today had he not done so.' The judge paused and took several gulps of water from the large glass. Then he continued:

'The defendant trusted his judgement in deciding to believe one son against the other. Our children don't always fulfil our hopes for them, but thankfully not many go on to become killers like Leo Grainger did.'

Judge Tovey paused again and seemed

to be deliberating, as though he was still uncertain of what he was about to announce as he reached for the water jug in front of him. The sound of the water being poured into the glass echoed around the otherwise silent courtroom. No one moved as they waited. This time the judge sipped from the glass and took a long look at Seth Grainger. Some eyes were fixed on the judge while others were on Seth Grainger, until the judge clasped his hands together and declared, 'It is the decision of this court that Seth Grainger be released from custody and I hope he will not spend the rest of his days regretting what he believed to be the right thing to do.'

The courtroom was filled with just about every emotion after the judge rose from his chair and left the court. Jarrod was devastated and quietly cursed the soft old judge. Sampson was elated, but when he shook hands with Seth Grainger he didn't detect any relief in a man who had just escaped a hanging or lengthy spell in prison.

24

Thomas Larkin fingered the small gold medal that he had been presented with by the president of the railroad company. It had been a proud day for his family, but that was nearly a year ago and now he had visibly changed from the man who had been reported as a hero in many of the national newspapers. His eyes were sunken through lack of sleep and his face was lined and drawn. He'd developed a bad cough, most likely caused by his recent habit of chain-smoking the cigarettes he rolled, using strong tobacco. He peered at the words on the inscription 'For Outstanding Bravery' and gave a 'tut' in disgust.

They had named a bridge after him following the untimely death of Stanmore Poulson, the former president of the railway company who had been killed by robbers who had boarded his special carriage. The guard who had been in the carriage had told Larkin that Poulson had behaved in his usual arrogant way and asked the robbers if they knew who he was. He had then threatened to have them hunted down and hanged. They had laughed in his face and one of them had shot him and thrown him out of the carriage while the train was moving at speed. His body was recovered the following day, but two of his limbs were missing and must have provided a meal for some wolves or other scavenger.

Poulson's death had been just three months after his wife and daughters had perished when their train had plunged off the Poulson Bridge that had been named after him. The bridge was renamed just last month and was now known as the Larkin Bridge in honour of Thomas Larkin's bravery in trying to save passengers when their train had plunged into the deep waters of the Crookham River. Larkin had been the only survivor, and Stanmore Poulson had thought it would be good publicity for the railroad if one of their employees was hailed as a hero.

Now Larkin could hardly look anyone in the eye, including his own wife, when they spoke about his bravery, because he knew he was a fraud and might have been responsible for the loss of a man's life that same day. He would never forget that poor pathetic man who didn't deserve to be left beside a railway track in a harsh terrain.

Larkin had been given the special title of Chief Guard, but he was wondering how long he could remain working. In recent months his work had deteriorated and he had become tetchy, mainly on account of his sleepless nights. When he did sleep he often had nightmares. Sometimes he saw the desperate, disfigured face of the man he had tricked into getting off the train. There were other images of buzzards pecking out the good eye of the poor wretch who had done nothing to deserve being abandoned in a deserted spot. Larkin had tried to console himself with the thought that the man would have drowned with the others had he remained on the train, but he couldn't. On the nights he didn't dream of the one-eyed man, he saw images of the agonized faces of Elizabeth Poulson and her daughters, trapped in the carriage. Sometimes he saw their dead and bloated faces even though they were all alive when he swam in the clear water of the Crookham River past their carriage window and saw them trying to break the glass and escape.

Larkin placed his medal inside a drawer and checked the time on his gold watch, which was another present from one of the many societies where he had appeared as a guest speaker.

'I'm just going for a walk, but I'll be back in time for dinner,' he had explained to his wife as she watched him tying the laces of his highly polished boots. He faced the mirror and went through his usual ritual of checking that his uniform was all buttoned up. Then he turned to his wife. She smoothed the lapels of his jacket with her hands and then picked up the clothes brush from the stand in the hallway and stroked it across his shoulders and down the back of his coat before giving the front a final brush.

'Now, don't you be late, my hero,' she said with a smile and stood on her toes like a ballet dancer, so she could kiss him on the cheek.

'I can smell dinner already and it's my favourite stew, so there's no chance of me being late,' he said, sounding enthusiastic, but food was the last thing on his mind.

She waited on the doorstep until he reached the end of the front path of the house and they exchanged waves as they had done on every occasion when they were parting even if only for a few hours.

* * *

When Larkin arrived at the railroad station he had an unexpected surprise. The train that was preparing to pull out of the station had J21 emblazoned on its side.

'Well, I'll be damned,' he muttered to himself. It was the same train that he had been assigned to when he'd first started work for the railroad company. He had been told that it was being scrapped, but the engine sounded as good as ever. He stayed on the platform and was quietly reminiscing to himself when Henry Coyne, the stationmaster, approached him.

'Just can't stay away, can you, Thomas?' Coyne said with a smile.

'Just out for a walk to work up an appetite before dinner, but I'm glad I got to see my old friend J21. What a surprise it was to see her.'

Coyne looked towards the old train that was about to go out of view and said, 'I was as surprised as you when she came rolling in, but she's still a beauty with all those brass fittings. I had a look around inside and she's as grand as ever. The driver told me that it might be used by the governor when he does a campaign tour of the state later this year. Anyway, I wanted to ask you a favour. Come along to the office and have a mug of my best coffee with a little touch of you know what in it to keep out that cold wind that's blowing in from the east. It'll be quiet here until the eight o'clock from Delmont Creek arrives, but I don't expect it to be on time.'

* * *

Thomas Larkin never arrived home for his dinner and he wasn't there the following day when a special letter arrived, inviting Mr and Mrs Thomas Larkin to meet the President of the United States at the White House in Washington DC. The invitation would never be accepted because Thomas Larkin was dead before his dinner was ready to be served. He had lain across the rail track near his home minutes before the train from Delmont Creek was due at that very spot and it was on time.

Henry Coyne told Larkin's widow that he'd been fine when he left his office after he'd just agreed to give a talk on the railroad at his son's school. He'd told Larkin that his son would have been so excited that a real hero would be coming to his school. He was certain that his son and some of his friends would want to work for the railways company because of the heroic feats of Thomas Larkin, whom he had been proud to have known.

25

It is three years since Bordon was the scene of the three trials that had been linked to the killing of young Donny Stokes and the other killings that followed it.

Seth made a recovery from his stroke, and although he never regained his full strength he never misses a weekly visit to the cemetery, and when he has attended the family graves he always visits the grave of Friedel who was buried on the same day as his son, Leo. He hadn't realized just how ambitious Friedel was, but looking back the signs were there and perhaps he should have handled him differently and not rushed his demotion from the foreman's position. Maybe if Friedel hadn't run into his son Scott so soon after being told the news about Scott coming back he might have come to terms with his disappointment. What if, is a question he poses frequently and tortures himself with.

People still talk about John Linton's strange relationship with his daughter that went beyond a parent's concern. It was as though he regarded his daughter's suitors as rivals. He had been warned not to return to the town when he came out of prison, because his business premises had been vandalized and accusing messages had been scrawled on the door. The warning would never be violated because he was battered to death with a urinal after an argument with another man whom he accused of stealing an artist's sketch of his daughter, Emma, when she was fourteen years old. Some folks say that you shouldn't speak ill of the dead, but there will always be some that do and there is little sympathy for John Linton.

Doc Bennett continues to weave his magic in patching up wounded cowboys and delivering babies. One of his greatest joys last year was seeing the delight on

Emma Linton's face when he had handed her the screaming baby boy that he had just pulled from her womb. He was honoured that the boy was to be named after him and expects to be attending Emma many more times as her family expands, because she has said that she wants lots and lots of babies. Emma Linton is still the subject of gossip amongst the busybody women folk and some have still not got over the shock of her marriage to the Reverend David Langford. The minister gave her comfort following her trauma and the jailing of her pa and a romance developed between them. Emma is blissfully happy, unaware that she is referred to by some as the Devil's daughter.

The doc will never forget seeing Seth Grainger sobbing in despair when he cradled his dead son on the floor of the saloon. Scott Granger had been drinking heavily and got involved in an argument with a group of men who were just passing through. Scott had been asking for trouble, a fight broke out and he was stabbed in the chest. Seth had been in town and was in the marshal's office chinwagging with his old friend Charlie Stephens when someone came running in and told the marshal that there was trouble over at the saloon and that Scott was in a bad way. The doc was attending to Scott when Seth entered the saloon and the doc's shake of the head told him that nothing could be done. Scott had given his pa a faint smile before he said in almost a whisper, 'I'm sorry, Pa. I lied. It was me who killed . . . ' Scott never uttered another word.

Seth Grainger had just discovered that both his sons had ridden the palomino the day Donny Stokes was killed and that perhaps he never did have one good son and one bad son.

THE END

We do hope that you have enjoyed reading this large print book.

Did you know that all of our titles are available for purchase?

We publish a wide range of high quality large print books including:
Romances, Mysteries, Classics
General Fiction
Non Fiction and Westerns

Special interest titles available in large print are:
The Little Oxford Dictionary
Music Book, Song Book
Hymn Book, Service Book

Also available from us courtesy of Oxford University Press:
Young Readers' Dictionary
(large print edition)
Young Readers' Thesaurus
(large print edition)

For further information or a free brochure, please contact us at:
Ulverscroft Large Print Books Ltd.,
The Green, Bradgate Road, Anstey,
Leicester, LE7 7FU, England.
Tel: (00 44) **0116 236 4325**
Fax: (00 44) **0116 234 0205**

DEAD END TRAIL

Tyler Hatch

Chet Rand is a decent, law-abiding man, but a forest fire wipes out his horse ranch, leaving him with nothing. However, when he comes across the outlaw Feeney — with a $1,100 reward on his head — it seems like a gift from heaven. Unfortunately, there are many shady characters in pursuit of the $12,000 Feeney has stolen — a more pressing matter than the bounty itself. So it's inevitable that when guns are drawn, blood will flow and men will die . . .

DUEL AT DEL NORTE

Ethan Flagg

Russ Wikeley settles in Del Norte, South Dakota, and after foiling a bank robbery he's persuaded to stand for sheriff in the town's elections. However, Diamond Jim Stoner, a gang boss, wants his own man to become sheriff and attempts to undermine Wikeley. When his plan backfires, he tries to frame his adversary for robbery and murder. Both men are determined . . . only one can be the victor in the final duel on the streets of Del Norte.

THE KILLING KIND

Lance Howard

Jim Bartlett thought he could put his past behind him and forge a new life in Texas, as a small ranch owner — but he was wrong . . . dead wrong. Someone from his past has followed him and is systematically trying to destroy his new life, piece by piece. With his friends and the woman he loves being threatened by a man who knows no remorse, Jim struggles desperately — not only to escape his past — but also to hold onto his life . . .